LPfic
Pai   Paine, Lauran.
            The apache kid

DATE DUE	RAF
MAR 16 2013	
APR 24 2015	
NOV 02 2015	
JAN 17 2017	

DEMCO, INC. 38-2931

the apache kid
(skee-bee-nan-ted)

the apache kid

(skee-bee-nan-ted)

LAURAN PAINE

SOUTH SIOUX CITY PUBLIC LIBRARY
2219 DAKOTA AVENUE
SOUTH SIOUX CITY, NE 68776

Thorndike Press • Chivers Press
Thorndike, Maine USA   Bath, Avon, England

This Large Print edition is published by Thorndike Press, USA and by Chivers Press, England.

Published in 1996 in the U.S. by arrangement with Golden West Literary Agency.

Published in 1996 in the U.K. by arrangement with Golden West Literary Agency.

U.S. Hardcover 0-7862-0652-7(Western Series Edition)
U.K. Hardcover 0-7451-4757-7(Chivers Large Print)
U.K. Softcover 0-7451-4758-5(Camden Large Print)

Copyright © 1996 by Lauran Paine
Copyright © 1950 by Lauran Paine in the British Commonwealth

All rights reserved.

Thorndike Large Print ® Western Series.

The text of this Large Print edition is unabridged.
Other aspects of the book may vary from the original edition.

Set in 16 pt. News Plantin by Minnie B. Raven.

Printed in Great Britain on permanent paper.

British Library Cataloguing in Publication Data available

Library of Congress Catalog Card Number: 95-91003
ISBN 0-7862-0652-7 (lg. print : hc)

the apache kid

(skee-bee-nan-ted)

CHAPTER ONE

In a sense, the personal war trail of the Apache Kid was a continuation of the age-old resistance of the Apache nation — its spirit, anyway — against those who would conquer an unconquerable people. There is a little irony, too, in the fact that, after Geronimo surrendered to General Nelson Miles in Skeleton Canyon, August, 1886, and the last concerted Apache effort to stay free collapsed, American historians are inclined to consider all aboriginal resistance in the United States at a final end. Well, the organised resistance *was* at an end, but fate had a joker up her sleeve. The Apaches, mightiest of Indian warriors, had still one more bolt to fire before the curtain was rung down on their valiant, stubborn battle for freedom. The Apache Kid.

And oddly, too, the Kid wasn't a recalcitrant Indian, either. Not until circumstances made him one. Possibly in this one instance there was justification in an outlaw becoming an outlaw; certainly there were inescapable circumstances that left him little alternative, plus the fact that other factors, forgotten now, contributed greatly toward making a good-natured, serious and intelligent young man, the last Apache to sear his name in blood across lower Arizona and Mexico.

In order to evaluate the Apache Kid fairly, one must know the country that sired him, the people, their traditions, spirit and beliefs, and the environment of hatred and distrust, contempt and disgust of their white conquerors. One must understand that Arizona and environs had no reason to sympathise with Apaches at any time, and in many places to this day despises them. Why? For the very elemental reason that no Apache warrior worthy of the name showed mercy to those who were invading his land, killing his people on sight and stamping out Apacheria forever, without quarter.

And on the other hand, the Apaches contributed to the demise of every white they could catch, with extremely few exceptions. Thus, the whites on both sides of the border can this day point to a black-bordered picture in the family album and say with justifiable bitterness: "That was Uncle Charley — killed by Apaches."

Basically, this mutual hatred, disguised, but very real nevertheless, was a basic and tangible part of the Apache Kid's world. There was another thing, too. The land. Apacheria, as it was in the Kid's day and still is to a large degree, is one of the least hospitable sectors of the arid South-West, with immense wastes, towering mountains, distances so vast they shimmer almost to the edges of Eternity, so little water and edible vegetation that civilised people avoid it to this day, and with a sanguinary stillness that is more menace than peacefulness.

In this portion of bland quietness death stalked by day and night, touching first this victim, then that one, and those who survived and came to thrive in it had to match it with a stamina rarely equalled on earth. A hardihood difficult to comprehend to-day, and an intelligence based on the very real understanding of a Nature hostile to all living things. In short, the Apaches, traditional dwellers of this deadly land, had to be even more deadly than Nature to stay alive, and more attuned to the harshness of eternal challenge to stay and multiply there.

When one studies the incredible battles, the amazing losses and the unequal contests that drenched this land with white and Apache blood, one seeks for a sound reason for the recurrent victories of the Indians, and finds it in the disparity between two kinds of people. One, brave to a fault, willing and determined, but bred away from the granite existence of such a land by generations of "civilised" progress, as opposed to the dark-skinned realists who could trot all day without water through a burning hell of desert, exhausting horses as easily as the uniformed whites that rode them, then turn and double back, still trotting afoot all night long, and arise the next dawn to sweep down on the valiant but thoroughly exhausted cavalrymen and fight them to a standstill, massacre those left standing, and retain enough energy to still slip away into the awaiting canyons and plan another foray.

Thus, the causes for hatred on both sides were well founded in the very differences between two kinds of people, and here too we find the reason for a time and era that could produce an Apache Kid. For "readjustment" never comes easily, and sometimes never at all, but while a conqueror is trying to batter down the "heathen" ways, the second generation is far worse off than the first generation. For nowhere is there a parallel for the Apache who grows up in a flux of fermenting, diametrically opposed, antagonistically confused, ideologies.

A good example is the Apache tribal law of yesteryear that decreed a murderer's life is at the disposal of the murdered's kinsmen. His nearest responsible relative, in fact. This, while definitely not even fundamentally akin to the white man's idea of legal arbitration, has obvious kernels of justice about it, and yet the Americans who ruled — with a heavy hand — the conquered Apaches subsequent to Geronimo's defeat, would look at the retaliator much as we would to-day. Two wrongs don't make a right, in essence, is the current judgment that opposes the Apache's way of justice.

An Indian named Toga-de-Chuz (or Togida-Chuz) was vieing for the hand of an Apache maiden with another Apache called by the white men "Rip."

This, in the early spring of 1860, at an Apacheria on the Gila River near the later site of the famous San Carlos Reservation, when the tribes were at, or near, the apex of their resistance against the encroaching whites.

Toga-de-Chuz was encouraged by second and third hand — probably deliberately planned and executed — remarks made by the girl. After Apache custom he slipped up to the hovel of the girl's parents, tied his horses outside and hid in the nearby brush until the maiden came out, untied the animals and led them to water. This unique acceptance of a fiancee could, and often was, prolonged coquettishly until the brave and the horses were in a state of near collapse. The more arrogant girls have been known to let a squirming Apache buck lie in groaning doubt for more than one day or night, which, while it worked understandable hardships on the Indian, was twice as hard on the horses.

The rivalry between Rip and Toga-de-Chuz was culminated with the acceptance of the latter, and a marriage followed, during which the indiscreet Toga-de-Chuz boasted of his victorious courtship. This, while in poor taste then as now, was a characteristic of Indian nature. One of the inexplicable inconsistencies that mark not only Apaches and Indians in general, but all humanity, so well. Warriors bragged often and upon the least encouragement. This was an expected and even admired form of personal aggrandisement designed to let the world know how courageous and clever each fighting buck was. It was accepted as a part of the Apache way of life.

Opposed to this Apache trait was the other, conflicting, characteristic that is also typically Apache — typically Indian, generally speaking. The astonishing lengths they will go for revenge, often waiting in silent patience for years on end, to repay a slight that other races would have shrugged off long before or forgotten entirely.

As a result of Toga-de-Chuz's ridicule of Rip before the other Apaches, and in view of his natural embarrassment, plus the typically Apache outlook of the man, it isn't any wonder that he seethed inwardly while saying nothing outwardly. Bearing the scorn of the victor with a stony look and a raging heart, Rip never forgot.

The Apache wars were in full scale during this time. Men like Mangus Coloradas, Cochise and the indomitable Geronimo, maligned and lied about to this day, led their fighting men across the vast South-West like phantom executioners. They struck deep into Mexico, then doubled back and terrorised Arizona, and before the smoke had died away from burning ranches, they were hundreds of miles away over in New Mexico, carrying murder, warfare and pillage wherever they went with a wiliness and blood-curdling ferocity never equalled before or since in American history. And Toga-de-Chuz rode with them, as did Rip.

While the tempo of the everlasting strife was near its peak, a son was born to Toga-de-Chuz's wife. This, in 1868. The lad was robust and sturdy from birth, thrived under typically adverse conditions that were Apache environment, and began his life close to the old San Carlos Agency where he was called "The Kid" by the rough, iron-hard and unscrupulous, often contemptuous, men, red and white, of the locality.

The Kid was pleasant, easily amused and inquisitive. He became, in time, a sort of mascot among the white men around San Carlos. Dark, with wide, close-set eyes, a high degree of intelligence and an ability to learn fast, the Kid wasn't unpleasant in disposition or appearance. In fact, according to Apache standards, he was rather good-looking.

In this confused time of jumbled beliefs, where not a few of the white men, Indian fighters, buffalo hunters, scouts and gunmen, settlers and adventurers, were more Indian than white, and where the Apaches had taints of Mexican culture laced through their own ideology, along with the newer, brasher American culture, the Kid grew up slowly, assimilating, weighing, understanding without knowing why, and remaining an Apache in heart.

So much an Apache that he eagerly studied the art of tracking, of reading signs where there were none visible to other than Apache eyes, and how to follow a trail where no white man on earth could even see one. This fascinating pastime consumed him until he was to become the finest tracker the South-West has ever known. More significant, this excellence in a lost art was to make him immune to pursuit through the only way one Apache could elude another Apache. A case of white men with their vastly superior arms and numbers throwing up their hands in defeat, and hiring "tame" Indians to track down their hostile kinsmen.

It was this very tactic that gave the Kid his start, for at the time his band was living in uneasy peace, Geronimo and a few other perennial hostiles were still scourging the land until the cries of the people back "in the States" were aroused to fury by the livid newspaper accounts of their fiendishness, thus spurring on an army already harassed and humiliated almost to distraction by failure after failure.

And into the maelstrom of conflict the superior trailing ability of the Apache Kid was drafted in 1885, when Al Seiber — stocky, taciturn, eminently fair, and a German emigrant who could and did shoot down his own Apache scouts when they disobeyed him — had need for the best of all Apache trackers. In his early 'teens, the Apache Kid, son of Toga-de-Chuz, with his natural bent for trailing that exceeded anything else, even the master trackers themselves, the Apaches, had ever seen, became a member of Company F, Indian Scouts, under the burly Al Seiber. He became his confidant, friend, superior and, in a way, the Apache Kid's idol; for of all the scathing contempt the white men had for Apaches —

especially the Army — Seiber alone stood out for them, and made it stick. Al Seiber said what he thought with a frank glance. The listener could disagree in either one of two accepted ways. With words or weapons. Seiber was never hasty, so he never backed down. This was the type of man an Indian could understand. Nothing complex, nothing intricate, about the Seiber type. Right was right and wrong was wrong. The Apache Kid came to lean heavily on Seiber, and not once was this confidence misplaced. In his own dour way, Al Seiber was the matrix against which the sixteen-year-old Apache Kid's spirit was first impressed to create the Apache renegade that would later become the most dreaded Indian to live on, long after the passing of Geronimo. To the Kid, right was right and the law was the law. Seiber taught him this. He never forgot it. If you had an obligation you discharged it. There were no half measures. The Apache Kid would remember, always.

In the meantime, he went out with other "tame" Apache trackers on Geronimo's trail. Stayed on it until Nan-tan Miles and his army worried Geronimo into final submission, and brought back the last great Apache war-leader a prisoner and as many of his people as didn't slip away, one and two at a time, the night before the last surrender.

Through all this the Apache Kid had opportunities galore to see how Apache prisoners were treated. He even saw that the army, making no distinction whatsoever, sent loyal "tame" Apaches into captivity and exile along with the very hostile elements the "tame" Indians had laboured so hard to run down for their new masters. He saw how soldiers killed women and children ("Kill the nits and you'll have no lice") and he came to know death intimately as it stalked bitterly through the Apache rancherias and soldier bivouacs, with no discrimination, and came to accept it as a part of life.

These were the formative years of a young man who, little known and unsung, was the last Apache fighting man, and it was during these years that Apache Kid learned not only the way of his own people but the ways of the white man as well, so that when he had to, later, he alone of all Apaches, could make fools of hundreds of older men with little effort.

It was also the time when no Indian — regardless — was considered equal to a white man under the laws of the land, and any Apache who fell afoul of the white man's jurisprudence was deemed guilty before trial, and had his guilt confirmed with as little waste of time as possible. The balance between a "good" Indian and a "bad" Indian was so slight that anyone could denounce an Apache. He would be speedily arrested, tried and convicted, sentenced and executed on evidence that to-day wouldn't get past a preliminary hearing. All this — to an Indian who more than likely knew little or no English — was first, last and always, "a savage," and was, therefore expendable — a "nit."

The Apache Kid, along with a white man named Tom Horn, later to achieve notoriety and be executed for killing a fourteen-year-old boy named Nickell, whom it has been proven recently he couldn't have killed, were with General Miles' forces when Geronimo was run down and taken.

Ironically, the Kid saw the last war-leader surrender. Saw him humbled and shipped into exile. And while he probably didn't breathe the universal sigh of relief that the white men did, he couldn't have known that he, himself, was to give the Apache Indians their last grim smile of triumph. For Geronimo was licked, but the Apache spirit never was, and the personification of that undying resistance was standing there in the lacy shade of scraggly little trees, beside Tom Horn and others: the Apache Kid.

The Kid was all Indian — all Apache, too — but he lived among both Apaches and whites as a member of Al Seiber's famous Apache Scouts. He was well liked, thought highly of and trusted thoroughly by both races.

It was by dint of application and diligence that the Apache Kid arose to the rank of sergeant among Seiber's scouts. He didn't go often to the tizwin parties of the Apaches, and had never been in any trouble as a result of breaching that delicate barrier between "superior" and "inferior" races. The months went by with routine scouting jobs, tracking down fugitives who, under the influence of Apache tizwin — Indian liquor distilled from the mescal plant: liquid dynamite — committed crimes that were punishable under the white man's code. His prowess as a tracker grew, as did the boy himself. Seiber acknowledged the Kid's natural aptitude for tracking many times. So did the other Apache scouts. Physically, the Apache Kid matured quickly, becoming powerful of shoulder, arm and leg, with the inherent stamina of his race and the basic courage of all men to whom life in a raw land is very real.

And, as the Kid had grown mature, strong and eagle-eyed, smart as a whip and above average in all the things of the two worlds, Toga-de-Chuz and Rip became middle-aged men. Supposedly beyond feeling the hot angers of early youth, and normally expected to have acquired the sagacity, the patient tolerance and forbearance of middle-aged men. Only they didn't. They were Apaches.

In the full of the moon at an Apache rancheria, or community camping area where the bands gathered, Toga-de-Chuz danced with the wild abandon of a youth. He drank tizwin the same way, laughed, joked, and shouted with the rest of the Apaches. That the making of tizwin had long been outlawed by the Americans was recognised, but so was raiding deep into Mexico. If one brought only a casual rebuke, why should the other bring more? The tizwin drunk was a gala affair, and during its peak of savage bedlam Toga-de-Chuz made his fatal blunder. He found his old whipping-boy among the bucks, and Rip came in for another hearty measure of derision. Whether Rip had been drinking or not isn't important, although he probably had, all things considered. What was important was that he arose, regarded Toga-de-Chuz for a long, still moment, then snarled a livid Spanish oath and lunged at him. Toga-de-Chuz, none too steady at best, reacted normally by ducking away. Rip went after him then, all the savage resentment of twenty years boiling up out of his craw, knife flashing, eyes awry with the wild hunger for blood, and Toga-de-Chuz was impeded in his manoeuvres to escape Rip's knife by the startled, wide-eyed watchers and, finally, in sobering desperation yanked at his own knife, turning to face the wolf-fury of Rip . . . too late. The knife came in like a flash of silver lightning, plunged past Toga-de-Chuz's breastbone and impaled his heart. Before Rip could shake off the limp weight, Toga-de-Chuz was dead, slumping against the killer and making small noises with his slack mouth, opening and closing.

The instant silence was in thick contrast to the drunken festivities of before. Apache minds reacted quickly. Toga-de-Chuz was dead by the hand of Rip. Tribal law decreed that Toga-de-Chuz's eldest son had not only the right, but the responsibility, of exacting punishment, and the son of the dead man was the most renowned tracker in the West. The Apache Kid.

The word travelled rapidly enough to the ranks of Seiber's scouts as all tragedy does, and in time, while Rip had made his hasty escape from the rancheria and the Agency, Toga-de-Chuz's son heard of his father's murder. For the first time in his life the terrible conflict within him had to be met head on. Tribal law decreed that he avenge his father, as indeed he wanted to do. But the white man's law said this was wrong, to take revenge, and yet most of his white friends, the men who lived as much by the law of a life for a life as any Indian ever had, sympathised and encouraged the Kid.

The Apaches themselves said nothing unless asked, then the answer was invariably the same. An Apache who wouldn't avenge his own father was a coward and worse. The dilemma was beyond solution for a white man of the time and place, the environment and the training. What chance had a youth?

Al Seiber, of course, heard the news almost as quickly as the Kid did. He knew Apaches better than any white man alive. He was, in fact, what has become termed a "White Indian." A man who weighs the two cultures and finds the Indian ideologies more adaptable in his case than the white. He sent for the Kid. Warned him that the white man's law under which they all lived now was against vengeance killings.

"If you revenge your father," he told the Kid in Spanish, "the white man's law will call you a murderer and an outlaw. You're a Sergeant of Scouts now, Kid. Don't jeopardise that."

The Kid was blank-faced. He thought in silence for a long time before he answered: "The white man's law is new, Apache law is ancient. If I don't avenge Toga-de-Chuz

I'll be an outcast."

"And if you do," blunt Al Seiber said grimly, "you'll be an outlaw. Another Apache renegade. Kid — listen to me. The white man's law will catch Rip. He will get what's coming to him. The law takes revenge, not the individual."

The Kid knew they were worlds apart in this instance, but also, he was very fond of the steel-nerved Seiber. He said nothing. Friendships are often destroyed by talk, and talk accomplishes nothing. Action counts. If he must lose this long-time friend, better to do it from a distance. Over Rip's body, maybe. He returned to the conical little hut that was his home at San Carlos Agency, and brooded.

The days went by. Seiber didn't talk to the Kid again. He said later there was nothing he could add to what he had already said. The decision, in any event, was the Kid's. Then Captain Francis Pierce, agent at San Carlos, needed a companion on a trip into the White Mountains, where he had business at Camp Apache, and called on his Chief of Scouts to go along. Seiber went, but prior to his departure he did the only thing a man could do to show the Apache Kid what he wanted, and how much he thought of his Apache tracker. By putting the Kid in charge of the Scouts in his absence, Seiber was showing — saying — that he wanted the Kid to be at San Carlos when he returned, and also, that he considered the Kid eminently trustworthy and law-abiding. It was a splendid gesture. One appreciated by all the Scouts, for by now everyone at San Carlos knew the Kid's dilemma. After that, Captain Pierce and Al Seiber left, and also after that, the hot-heads among the Apache bucks converged on the Kid and urged him not to sacrifice his standing among the Indians by ignoring his tribal responsibilities. In short, they offered to go with him in his search for Rip, the murderer. This urging came also from the very Scouts under him, supposedly models of "tame" Apaches like he was. He went, taking with him less than a half-dozen Apaches. The seed was sown; the die was cast. The name Apache Kid, which, heretofore, had been a designation for a young Apache Indian, was soon to assume the sinister character of all Westerners before and since who have been called The Kid. Billy the Kid, Kid Curry, the Sundance Kid. Killers all. Add to that now the Apache Kid.

The Kid led his bronco bucks on a trail nearly a month old, but recognition of the justice of his mission made it easy enough to find old Rip. Apaches en route nodded approval and pointed out the way. This was no case for a fabulous tracker after all: just an avenger.

When the Kid found Rip the older man was in his frugal encampment beside the Arivaipa Creek. By the time he heard the coming of death, the Kid had placed his companions at strategic points, still astride, while he himself went forward afoot unnoticed until he was almost behind Rip, then the old buck leapt up and whirled, but it was too late. The Kid looked into that seamed, bitter face, read hatred and resignation there, and shot Rip to death where he crouched. Nothing dramatic happened. Just two Apaches glaring across a breach that was murder, Indian ferocity and tradition, with the Kid's gun acting as sole arbiter.

Rip was left where he fell, his horses were turned loose, nothing else was touched, and the Apache Kid went back to his horse, swung up, motioned in his friends and told them that they were now renegade Apaches, the scourge of all whites. They rode for the impregnable mountains of ancient Apacheria, where the sighing wind in the treetops made the only sounds now, since Geronimo had surrendered. There, once more, the spirit that drove other fighting Apaches, since time immemorial, lived again in the rancheria of the Apache Kid and his pitiful little band of defiant bucks. They became forerunners of other little groupings of hold-outs that spit in the teeth of "civilisation" to this very day, preferring the Old Way of Apacheria to the new way of America.

Not the last and certainly not the first little clutch of Apaches to hurl defiance at the massed hosts of a mighty nation, the Apache Kid was to become a classic as an example of indomitable resistance against enforced domination, and to stand head and shoulders above all others since, that have followed his example down across the years.

While the Kid was prudently awaiting to gauge San Carlos' reaction to his deed, he and the other bucks hunted, fished, stole a few fresh horses, and in general re-lived the old life and found it wonderfully good. It is unique, and yet typical of the Kid, that he scorned hiding Rip's carcass, or making any attempt to conceal his crime — which he didn't consider a crime at all — and thus, in due course of time, Rip's body was found and the news went abroad.

Al Seiber heard it back at San Carlos, but he didn't need confirmation, anyway. The Kid wasn't at the Agency when he got back. Al Seiber knew Apaches; he knew what had happened as surely as though he had seen it occur. Listening to the account of the finding of old Rip's coyote-mangled, buzzard-plucked remains, he sat glumly out in front of his tent and stared implacably over the sink of pestilence that was San Carlos Agency, a place where the sun drained energy, and often life itself, from everything, as far as a man could see. He spat against the packed earth and swore to himself. It wasn't so much that he felt any betrayal of trust. That wasn't it at all. What bothered the burly frontiersman was that the Kid was his best scout. Not just his best tracker and one of the best shots on the Agency, but a youth who had often collaborated with him on the trail of criminals. A friend, in short, of whom he thought very highly.

Seiber knew why the Kid had "gone out." He was a "White Indian," too. What the Kid had done, Al Seiber would have done the same way. He didn't altogether agree with the white man's law — but he had sworn to uphold it, and so had the Apache Kid. There was a core of something called progress that had been forsworn in favour of the old way which was the best, perhaps, but wasn't any longer recognised as such. Seiber was only a little less confused in his thinking than the Kid had been — still was — but he knew one thing with absolute certainty. The Apache Kid was now an outlaw. One of the wraith-like phantom Apaches who stood beyond the pale; a bronco buck; a renegade; an Apache who had "gone out."

Al sent for a shady Apache who was suspected of having joined wild bunches now and then when the thralldom of San Carlos weighed too heavily and the young hot-heads leapt on their horses and cut a swath of terror into neighbouring Mexico. He knew this buck could and would find the Kid.

"Tell him to come in. I want to talk to him."

That was all the message Seiber sent. He didn't say whether the Kid would be arrested or not. Just to come in; they would talk. There is no better indication of the feeling each had for the other than the fact that on the first day of June, 1887, the Apache Kid and his little band, swelled somewhat by other bronco bucks and a few bored "tame" Indians from San Carlos, came riding slowly into the Agency, heading straight for Al Seiber's tent.

No one can deny that several of the renegades had been drinking. That others were openly riding with their carbines cradled across their laps and that all were ready for whatever happened, truculent even, in their crossed glances with American soldiers and Indian policemen.

Captain Pierce, a prudent man, was nearby. Sensing tragedy in the making, he hastened to Seiber's side, watching the hard-eyed bucks rein up and sit there stoically, granite eyed and waiting. Turning, the Captain spoke clearly to his chief of scouts.

"Mr. Seiber — have them disarmed."

Al didn't reply. He looked at the Kid, met his glance squarely for a long while, then let his glance drift over the other Indians behind him. He also saw Apaches drifting up from over the Agency. These, for the most part, were afoot, but a few were on horseback. There were guns visible among the "tame" Indians, too. He looked back at the Kid again.

"Kid — get down and take their guns. Bring them over here and put them on the ground."

The Kid dismounted and walked among his followers, hardly speaking. The Apaches handed over their guns, if not with grace at least without refusal. Then the Kid carried the load of weapons over by Al Seiber and dumped them on the ground. Seiber's face was expressionless. He stared at the jumbled weapons and spoke again without looking up from them.

"Take your men and report in over at the guardhouse, Kid."

Then and there the drama might have ended. Undoubtedly would have, except for the fight Al Seiber would have put up to save his protege from execution as a murderer. But it wasn't to end that way — nothing as spectacular as the career of the Apache Kid could have been culminated so ignobly. Not when the West was young.

Among the antagonistic "tame" Apaches, always an undependable quotient at best, was a squatty Apache called Curley. He was in the crowd of watchers that had accumulated around the mounted renegades. Just exactly what he held against Al Seiber is not known now, but he had a gun in his hand, concealed by his shirt-tail. When the Kid moved away from the chief of scouts, preparatory to obeying Seiber's command, Curley raised the gun too fast for good aim and fired it. With a roar of wrath, Al Seiber flung himself backwards into his tent where his own guns lay, snatched up one and emerged into the pandemonium and fired a snap shot at a nearby Apache who was waving a gun, and killed the man instantly.

But the damage had been done. Apaches fought to get away from the place. Those on horseback rode over those afoot, and when the bedlam and dust had settled down, the Apache Kid, his mounted followers, and not less than six other "tame" Apaches had fled overland as fast as their horses could go, confused and bewildered, but alive and thankful for that, not knowing just what had happened, nor staying around to find out when all their own arms were in a heap before Seiber's tent.

The die was irrevocably cast now. The renegades went first in search of guns. In this particular they were successful, although the men who gave up their firearms were left dead, too. The Kid struck like lightning now. He no longer vacillated. At Atchley's ranch his band "exchanged" horses, leaving their worn-out mounts, head down, foamy and finished, in the place of fresh, strong animals. Farther on Bill Diehl, a lone miner, made the mistake of drawing his gun when he saw the Apaches racing toward him on their new horses. He died where he took his stand, was robbed as a matter of course, and the Kid then swung up the San Pedro river leading his little war party towards the hills. Here he found another pair of guns for his men — belted to the waist and in the saddle-scabbard of one Will Grace. These were acquired, Grace left sprawled and lifeless, and now the Indians turned south, riding for Mexico, the only place in the locality where they could find safety for a while.

But this wasn't the Arizona of Geronimo's earlier forays. This was the new West of hard riding, straight shooting, cowmen and settlers; a land where soldiers had stayed long enough now to be acclimatised. A place where wireless played its priceless role in conquest. A country of second generation white Arizonans, who brought with them their inherited intelligence and coupled it to their environmental background so that here, for the first time, the Apaches had nearly an equal, in fighting whites.

And the news spread like wildfire, too. Geronimo was still a name used by the Mexicans — and sometimes the whites as well — to frighten children into obedience. The very name "Apache!" was like an icicle down one's back. So, with the wires singing their urgent song of death and Apache violence once more, the land roused itself from the summer stupor and saddled up, snatched down carbines, rekindled slumbering fires of hatred for anything Apache, and took to the trail.

The soldiers went abroad en masse. Still smarting under the disgrace of Geronimo, the Army used its costly experience to good advantage. Patrols raced for the border, threw out an inflexible cordon and held it athwart the route of the Apache Kid. He was bottled up very effectively and didn't even know it until he galloped to within a thousand yards of a moving patrol, skidded to a halt and watched the vastly superior cavalry company riding their beat.

The Kid turned back, probed for an opening into Mexico farther up country, found just how completely the Army had digested the lessons it had learned from Geronimo, and, fearing now to linger, rode helter skelter back up toward San Carlos again — but fate was in earnest this time. The Kid's trail was cut by a troop of cavalry under Lieutenant Frank Johnson, taken up with a whoop by Johnson's "tame" Apache scouts, and the race began. The Kid could see his pursuers and knew he couldn't hope to evade them very long. His horses — or rather Bill Atchley's horses — were bushed. The cavalrymen were freshly astride. Desperately, the Kid made it for the Rincon Mountains, hoping for a chance to utilise these age-old retreats of harassed Apaches since the first Indian raider got up onto a horse, and here Johnson overtook him. Flinging themselves from the spent animals, the Kid's men dropped down against the flaky ground to give battle, but here too, he was badly out-manoeuvred. The cavalrymen had cover and fire-power. They threw a withering blast into the exposed Indians and killed two of the Kid's band outright. The Kid saw extermination staring him in the face. He ordered his men to get astride again, propped up the dead Apaches so as to appear that they were still aiming their guns, swung up and led the balance of his men in a roundabout way back to — of all places — the San Carlos Agency.

Here, there was the slimmest chance that the "tame" Indians wouldn't betray him. It was almost a worthless gamble. He knew it, but he also knew that at San Carlos the pressure wasn't as great as elsewhere, and here too, there might be food and rest for a brief spell. Still, the Kid wasn't always in one place, either. He was in the home of his father-in-law, Eskim-in-zim, when the news came that a freighter who was known as a whiskey-peddler, was slashed to death in his trading camp on the upper San Carlos river, about fifteen miles away, and that the Apache Kid had done the deed. There was considerable head shaking over this accusation, but the Apaches in general, and the Kid in particular, hadn't yet become aware that his name lent itself admirably to tongue, when there was anything in the way of an unsolved crime that just had to be hastily solved. Thus, his notoriety, like that of so many outlaws, began to acquire that historic dust that gathers invariably and obscures the real man, and his deeds, beyond it.

Newspapers were aided by anti-Apache whites, of which there was a tremendous majority, not just in Arizona, either; as well as by out and out liars, and by gifted exaggerators, which is another name for newsmen in search of something vivid — then as now —

and gradually the fame of the Apache Kid, actually with no more foundation than two, possibly three, actual killings to date, began to blossom forth, festooned with gory garlands such as the impossible affair of the liquor-peddler on the upper San Carlos.

But the Kid's resentment didn't blind him either. He had to move again. He didn't take Eskim-in-zim's daughter with him then. He who would travel fastest must needs travel alone. Perhaps there were chivalric inhibitions here, but this was an Apache, not a Sir Lancelot. The difference is vast to those who understand them — romanticists aside. But in the interim the land was over-run with horsemen. Cowboys, ranchers, even fools who thought to collect his black scalp, had come from the East. Men the Apache Kid scorned killing they were so patently ridiculous. But the Army wasn't contemptible, and it was everywhere, like blades of grass, sprouting out of the rimrocks, the mountains and the very desert itself.

The Kid's followers, as few as ever, raced for the old strongholds of their people — only to discover that these wily soldiers were there ahead of them. They fled back down the San Pedro again for Mexico and once again were turned back. They hid by day and foraged by night, but the horse herds were guarded by hair-tempered cowboys now, and every house in the land seemed to have squads of soldiers or bristling stockmen on guard day and night in overwhelming numbers.

The Apache Kid was through with the elementary education of his life as a renegade now. He had applied the hereditary tactics of his people, and found them out-moded. Geronimo's strategy was useless, as was Juan Jose's and Cochise's. This was a new West; a new Arizona, and a way of life that the old-timers couldn't have coped with. The Apache Kid, lean as a wolf, sun-blackened, his ribs showing and his eyes sunken back into his skull, made the bitter discovery that it was not just tracking any more, that would overtake the lawless. It was the white man's progress. His growth and strength — and experience — in the old land. The Kid was licked and knew it.

But he wasn't beaten into submission, or made lethargic either. He didn't ride out on his bony nag and offer his gun to the first savage-eyed cowboy or soldier he saw, for the white man's law that wouldn't avenge his father was more than willing to sanction his own murder at the hands of any white man who was fortunate enough to align the Apache Kid over rifle sights. He sent in the least known of his bronkos with an offer to surrender and take his medicine, if he would be guaranteed passage across the desert to San Carlos.

Al Seiber and Captain Fran Pierce insisted he was entitled to this. Together, a bad pair to cross, they overrode the violent objections of the Army and the ranchers alike, warned against any incipient lawlessness, such as a lynching, backed it up with solemn promises that they would personally repay any white man who defied their edicts, then sent the Kid word he could come in safely. He did, and so ended another phase in the poignant story of a young Apache caught in a maelstrom of puzzlement, conflict and bewilderment that no one, white man or Indian, could or ever did, unravel, until time smoothed over the differences between two diametrically opposed races, but hasn't yet solved any of their problems.

CHAPTER TWO

The Kid surrendered to the Army, for he was an Army employee. This excited vast resentment among the civilian population of Arizona, but Captain Pierce, backed up and encouraged by a growling, bellicose Al Seiber, made it stick. The Apache Kid was an enlisted man of the United States Army, as were several of his cohorts. The civil courts could do what they wished — they would not get a chance to try Federal prisoners.

While Arizona seethed, the Army had a court martial hearing. The Apache Kid and enlisted companions were found guilty of desertion and sentenced to prison. They went stoney-eyed, to atone for subsequent acts arising from the one act they didn't believe was wrong at all. The killing of old Rip.

But the South-West wasn't Washington. The name "Apache" didn't have the same terror attached to it in the District of Columbia that it had at places like Globe and Tombstone, Galeyville and Tucson. The Apache Kid's case was reviewed by the military in Washington, then was handed over for Presidential study, with the stunning result that President Grover Cleveland reversed the Army verdict, found that the conditions and circumstances under which the Kid had deserted were extenuating enough to warrant a pardon, and the Kid was set loose again.

This was the second time, then, that Fate opened up a way for the Kid to fit himself back into his old life. The first time his intentions had been circumvented by a fool of an Indian named Curley, who shot Al Seiber in the ankle, the ball emerging some way from the bottom of his foot, leaving an awesome hole that never healed; became a running sore that had to be dressed twice daily to the end of his life.

Now the Kid was exonerated and supposedly eligible for reinstatement as an "honorary American" again, but Arizona still had its legal fangs bared. Here was an Apache being pardoned. In fact, here was a renegade Indian that had never been tried for the murders he had committed at all. The Kid was arrested on the charge of murder, among other things, which included wilful destruction of property, horse stealing, and a lot of crimes he couldn't possibly have committed if he had been triplets.

Nor was he alone. In all, eight of his former friends were caught and taken to Globe with him, where they were arraigned before one Judge Joseph Kibbey, in the District Court at Globe, Gila County, Arizona.

The trial was a farce. There was absolutely no creditable evidence presented to link any of those Indians to the crimes committed, although the Indians admitted the killings of two prospectors. Then, on the 18th of October, 1889, a verdict of guilty of murder in the first degree was handed down, which was — so benevolently — altered to seven years of hard labour in the old territorial prison at Yuma, Arizona, a place where more men died of exposure and dysentery than any other similar institution in the history of the old West. But the most ironic part of the sentencing was that, having insufficient evidence of any of the crimes to make them stick, even of the acknowledged killings of Grace and Diehl, the Apache Kid and co-defendants were found guilty of killing the whiskey-peddler on the upper San Carlos River, which the Kid didn't and couldn't have had a hand in.

Prior to being hauled to the Yuma prison, the Kid and his fellow felons were confined at Globe, until such a time as their transport could be arranged. This finally was taken care of on the first of November, at which time Sheriff Glenn Reynolds and one deputy, a man named William Holmes, but bearing the nickname of "Hunky Dory," completed stage connections and loaded their charges aboard. Here, one of those unique happenings that consistently appear along the route through life, and history, stands out. Tom Horn was Sheriff Reynolds' deputy, like Holmes. The difference between the two deputies was vast, however, for Tom Horn, aside from a good knowledge of Spanish, plus a smattering of Apache, was also a top-notch cowboy at a time when every horseman west of the Missouri competed, and all were good.

As a result of Tom Horn's vaunted ability as a roper he and another rider had a contest slated for the show at Phoenix, and the Sheriff gave Tom time off to compete. For this reason, Horn wasn't on the stage that bore the Apaches out of Globe, on the long, twisting, hilly road to Yuma. So, Tom Horn lived to equal the Apache Kid for notoriety, and in his place the second-stringer, Hunky Dory Holmes, didn't.

The Kid and companions, plus one slight, wiry Mexican horse thief named Jesus Aviota, were loaded into 'Gene Middleton's weathered old Concord stage, shackled together, glum and dour faced, and the trip was started.

The first day they made Riverside, on the Gila River, some forty odd miles from Globe, and here they were put up for the night with ample volunteer guards to relieve the law officers of their responsibility and enable them to sleep. The following day they struck out again early in the morning. It was a bitterly cold morning. Both Sheriff Reynolds and Deputy Holmes wore overcoats. Nor did they remove them even after they had to get down and walk behind the stage, with their charges, because the load was too heavy, the horses too tired after dragging the Concord across a sandy wash, and the trail ahead too steep for the fatigued animals.

The driver, 'Gene Middleton, told Sheriff Reynolds he could leave the Apache Kid and another buck named Say-ez, inside, which was done, then the balance of the Indians were unloaded and motioned to walk along up the hill behind the coach. Several Apaches preceded the Sheriff, who had Holmes beside him. Trudging along behind Holmes and Reynolds, heads down, manacled and dispirited, came the rest of the prisoners. The Mexican horse thief was far in the lead. The stage road had a bend just ahead around which 'Gene Middleton had disappeared with his coach and six.

Sheriff Reynolds dropped back a little, watched the following Apaches coming, and let a brace of them pass him before he resumed his own ascent of the steep trail. There were now two Apaches in front, and two behind Sheriff Reynolds, who was using his carbine as a sort of cane. At the bend in the road, this latter group was hidden from sight of Deputy Holmes. As though by a pre-arranged signal, one of the prisoners behind Reynolds leaped forward, swung his arms up and over the Sheriff's head and the handcuffs did what the Indian probably couldn't have done by himself. They pinioned Sheriff Glenn Reynolds in a grip of steel that forced his arms to his sides and held them there. The Sheriff, seeing himself helpless, bawled out to Hunky Dory Holmes. The deputy turned, bringing up his own carbine, and was instantly set upon by two of the Apaches in his own forward group. One of those absolutely unexpected events then occurred that are ironic, to say the least. Holmes had a heart attack, slumped forward unconscious, and caused not only his own death by so doing, but also the Sheriff's.

Manacled though they were, the prisoners tore away the deputy's carbine and hand-gun. One Indian shot Hunky Dory where he lay, while the man with the carbine jumped clear of the obstruction that hid Reynolds from sight, shoved the gun against the Sheriff's neck and pulled the trigger. Both lawmen were killed almost instantly.

In the furore, 'Gene Middleton heard the

shots, set his hand-brake, snatched out his six-gun, cocked it and aimed at the Apache Kid and Say-ez. The latter yelled in English: "Don't shoot; we're not in it!"

Middleton didn't shoot, although that had been his intention, and the Kid sat there staring at him, acknowledging that the driver was sparing them when actually they shouldn't have expected it. Say-ez and the Kid were no more "in it" than the Mexican horse thief. Jesus Aviota, manacles notwithstanding, was streaking it like a rabbit, across the hillside, anxious to put as many yards between his hide and the bronko Apaches as he could. He must have been quite a runner at that.

Middleton craned his head to see down the road over the top of the stage. A carbine thundered and Middleton was knocked off his high seat with blood gushing into his eyes and over his face. The horses jumped out in a stampede at the sudden shot, jerked Middleton loose of the coach and left him in the roadway. The Kid kicked open the stage door and leaped out, as did Say-ez, following the Kid's example. It took only a matter of minutes for the killers to take the dead Sheriff's keys, extricate themselves from the manacles and search the fallen men for additional guns. Then one of the excited bucks raced back to where Middleton was lying and pressed his gun into the stage driver's face and was in the act of cocking the gun when the Apache Kid walked up.

"Leave him alone," he said in Spanish, "he's had enough."

"But maybe he's alive."

"No. Look at that blood; he's dead. Leave him alone." The Kid knew 'Gene Middleton wasn't dead. He had seen his nostrils contract with the effort of breathing. Repayment, no doubt, for sparing two lives shortly before, when he could have taken them very easily. 'Gene Middleton died ten years later, in the summer of '99, and to the day of his demise, carried a livid scar below his jaw where a bronko Apache buck had blasted him off his Concord coach the day the Apache Kid and his cohorts escaped. Hunky Dory Holmes lay beside Sheriff Glenn Reynolds, stripped of their wallets, watches, six-guns and carbines.

The Kid fled astride after catching the coach horses, cutting them out, mounting two men on two horses and leading the little band of renegades south toward the San Pedro in a race against time. He made the men ride hard, too. His lesson of defeat prior to surrendering before, was fresh in his mind. As soon as someone came along and found the dead men and the abandoned stage, the talking wires would be at work spanning the desert again.

While the Kid's band rode for the San Pedro though, no travellers happened along, and probably that alone saved the Indians from immediate pursuit and almost certain capture.

Jesus Aviota finally stumbled into the yard of a rancher and told what had happened. But even Aviota's story wasn't the revelation that sent the frontier into a frenzy of action. It was the superhuman trek of bloody, staggering, often crawling on all fours, frequently unconscious, bled-out and nearly dead 'Gene Middleton who eventually made his way to town and told the story of the double killings before he slumped over and passed out for a long, long time.

By then, however, the Kid's band was safe. Later, a posse of murderous tempered cowboys and townsmen tracked the Indians to the river, only to discover that they had split up like a covey of quail — which they emulated exactly, at times like these — and each buck rode a separate trail to some unknown rendezvous.

There would be no turning back this time. The Kid knew it, Al Seiber and Captain Pierce knew it, and so did every gun-bearing cowboy who rode with his eyes slitted, wolf-like and wary, now. This would be war to extinction one way or the other, and until the bronkos were taken or killed no rider would be safe on the roads or cow ranges.

The south-west shuddered once more, for Apaches rode through the night again, the dull thunder of their racing horses a dirge of death. It wasn't the Apache Kid so much as every zealous or resentful, or just plain excitement-hungry, Indian who used the Kid's spectacular escape and subsequent good fortune in not being re-taken, as a signal to let off steam.

Stories of atrocities, of besieged ranches in the lonely far reaches of Arizona, New Mexico and Old Mexico, of dead men beside the trails, and of wanton murders and fiendish destruction, magnified at each telling, resurrected all the old terror that had been put to rest with Geronimo's surrender. And the Apache Kid was pictured as leading an almost messianic existence. Being reported at a dozen different places at the same time, now leading a tizwin frenzied host of hundreds, now leading his actual band of less than a dozen hard-riding renegades. The story of his brutality and fury became a legend that no one can delve into to-day without a sense of hopelessness, as far as separating the wheat from the chaff is concerned. But then, in 1889, just the word "Apache" was enough. All the old stories were brought out, dusted off and put back into active circulation. Only now it was always "the Apache Kid done that, sure as hell. It's his handiwork; I'd know it anywhere."

But the Apache Kid actually, during this time, did little more than acquire the best horses he could find, plenty of guns and ammunition, and watch his back trail constantly. There would be no surrendering this time. He knew it, and turned all his efforts and capabilities toward staying a free man. His success can best be measured in what happened hereafter. The elementary schooling over with, the Apache Kid was never again to surrender. As clever as an old coyote, he brought into play a knowledge vastly superior to what any other south-western renegade buck ever possessed. Raised as much by whites as by Indians, he knew the ways of both. Thusly equipped, an Apache was now to face the frontier as an equal to those who were storming over the land after him. Let us see who is to be victorious this time!

The Kid's close collaborator, one Pash-law-ta, and his old friend Say-ez, led the band that fluctuated with the coming and going of fighting Apaches under the loosest of discipline, but probably never numbered over ten renegades, south into Mexico. Here, the terror was greatest, for the Mexicans had learned generations before the coming of the Americans that Apaches were wolves in human form. They fled at the first rumour of Apaches on the loose again. Whether it was the Apache Kid and eight men, or Geronimo and fifty fighters, made no difference. It was armed, ravening Apaches. That was enough.

The Kid's men made Mexico their headquarters for a comfortable stay, and raided leisurely. Abandoned ranches, complete with food, livestock, even furniture and clothing, saddlery, good horses and hastily-hidden, pitiful little hoards of money were found. During this stay south of the border there was very little killing done. There was no need for it.

The Mexican guerilla soldiers, a pale imitation of the Apaches in tactics and strategy, simply avoided the invested areas in droves. And while the idyllic period was at its heights, back across the line in Arizona Al Seiber had his mind diverted from the frenzy that had sent Army and civilian riders lashing out blindly in every direction, having a heyday of hangings, and not a little looting also, by an incident that lent itself to his ponderous mind as a very subtle way of enticing the Kid into gun range, for, while Al had sympathised with Apache Kid up to the very day he embarked for Yuma's infamous old prison, he reacted violently and adversely to 'Gene Middleton's story of the brutal slaying of Holmes and Sheriff Reynolds.

Two of Seiber's Apache scouts had gone to

a tizwin drunk far back in the hills, using the usual excuses for getting away, and while there, these two bucks, called Josh and Nosey, while attending to and adding unto, the festivities, which became more violent as time — and tizwin — went by, until the affair, as always, culminated in one terrific fight in which everyone joined in, and the unlucky ones were normally secretly buried without trace when the Indians sobered up, Nosey became embroiled in an argument over a horse with another Apache. This wasn't unusual, either, since horse ownership was a nebulous thing that ante-dated most arguments by rarely more than one or two dark nights, and during the verbal sparring, Nosey's antagonist called in a friend, who instantly sided with Nosey's opposite, which put drunk Nosey at some disadvantage. In order to rather equalise things, Nosey then called upon Josh, his fellow scout, and after this the affair went from bad to worse until knives were bared. Nosey killed his man. This ended the argument very effectively and abruptly. The two scouts got to their horses and rode away, leaving the deceased where he lay.

Aside from tribal retribution which would pursue the killers, there was the inescapable fact that too many "tame" Apaches had witnessed the killing for it to be kept secret for long. Nor was it. While Nosey and Josh were fleeing into the convenient and ever-waiting stronghold of all Apaches, the mountains around Apacheria, Al Seiber heard the story several times, compared notes and came to the conclusion that Nosey and Josh were murderers under the white man's law. Rarely did an Apache ever kill in self-defence. A white man very often did, but not an Apache.

Seiber pondered, then came up with a simple solution that was typical of him. He sent word via an Apache scout of his command, known to be a close friend of the two killers, that if they would manoeuver the Apache Kid and his band into a position where they could be attacked by the Army successfully, Nosey and Josh would be not only forgiven their killing but be reinstated in his Apache scouts.

But the two Indians, after discussing the thing at great length with the man who brought them the message, decided that getting a man as smart as the Apache Kid into an ambush just wasn't feasible. Nor was it, either. Still, Josh and Nosey had no alternative but to try. They sent word back to Al Seiber of their good intentions and struck out, seeking sign of the Kid's band.

The Kid was freshly back from Mexico, where he had gained considerable weight. His little band was encamped in the uplands, relaxing, under the leadership of Say-ez, while the Kid himself had gone again to see his wife on the San Carlos Reservation, loaded with presents for the girl.

Say-ez had scouts out; thus, when Nosey and Josh were seen approaching, they were watched carefully for treachery, the main weapon the white man had instilled to his advantage among all the Apaches now, was the only weapon he could use successfully against recalcitrants. Even after the two killers were in the renegade camp and told of their crime, Say-ez was not completely convinced. In the first place, both Nosey and Josh were known as among the best men Seiber had; were one hundred per cent loyal to their leader, and had never — except for tizwin drunks — championed the cause of any sore-head Apaches. On top of this, just back from Mexico and not yet in touch with their friends, informers and suppliers at San Carlos, there was nothing known of the actual killing except what Josh and Nosey said.

In view of this, the two renegades were accepted with lingering doubts which were never completely dispelled, although they were allayed by the willingness with which Nosey and Josh went along and participated in several horse raids, during which one or two cowboys, caught far out on the range, were shot down and killed.

Nosey and Josh played their parts well during the absence of the Kid. So well, in fact, that one morning, an hour or two before dawn, when the other six renegades under Say-ez were sleeping soundly in their blankets, Nosey aroused Josh, and both bucks sat up, unlimbered their six-guns and shot every buck to death where they lay. All except Say-ez himself, who, badly wounded, leapt up and ran for his life into the tree-studded brakes around the camp, and escaped — for a while, anyway.

Say-ez had two bullets of large calibre in him. He bled badly, leaving a trail that even a white man could follow. Collapsing near a little spring, where he gulped water, he was found two days later, more dead than alive, fly-blown and semi-delirious; was tied on to a horse and taken to Globe, tried, convicted and sentenced to imprisonment at the old Yuma penitentiary, where he escaped by dying as a result of his two unattended wounds.

But Nosey, evidently a chary character, decapitated Pash-law-ta, took the horses of the other bucks, plus their weapons, and in company with Josh rode all the way back to San Carlos and didn't rein up until they were outside Seiber's tent. When Al limped out and saw them, Nosey dismounted, untied the breech-clout he had stripped from Pash-law-ta, from behind his saddle, hunkered in the dust and rolled out the head. Seiber was satisfied that Nosey and Josh had done what they claimed. Wiped out the Kid's band — but not the Kid. The head was good evidence, as were the horses and guns. He had both renegades pardoned and reinstated in his Apache scouts. Also — the most valuable thing Nosey and Josh brought back to Seiber — was the fact that the Apache Kid was even then right under the nose of the very authorities, who were frothing at the mouth over their sterile search for the wanted man in the even more sterile fastnesses of the desert country. Seiber digested this intelligence with resentment. White man treachery, deliberately encouraged among the Apaches until no Indian could be sure that whatever he did wouldn't be whispered into the Army's long ear, had backfired a little. The Kid had been at San Carlos for several weeks, and no Indian had disclosed his presence. Seiber, angry and chagrined, went to the Army and told them where the Kid probably could be found — in the camp of Eskim-in-zim. But again, the Kid's popularity twisted the white man's deceit. He was warned in ample time to escape. When the troop of smartly-riding cavalrymen surrounded Eskim-in-zim's corrals and *jacal*, the

Apache Kid had long since ridden away. More furious than ever, the Army made threats against the Kid's wife and father-in-law, and went away in disgruntled wrath.

But the Kid's visit to San Carlos hadn't been confined to connubial bliss, either. He had acquired a good pair of field glasses, plus the news of interest on the American side of the line, and when the wildfire story of the cold-blooded slaughter of his friends, Pash-law-ta, Say-ez and the others, spread across Apacheria, he heard it stoically and bowed before the original tenet of survival that had always kept him a solitary man. He would not recruit more warriors. This was to be a private war between Apache Kid and the Americans. If other Apaches came to him he would not turn them away, but he wouldn't depend on them as allies, nor encourage them either.

Out of this black deed, too, arose the Apache Kid's understanding that his people were not the old Apaches any longer. They were a race of men reduced to forked-tongued dealing with their own kind. Employers of the very treachery that had first soured them against the double-dealing Mexicans and Americans. He could not trust anyone, Apaches included, any more.

Eskim-in-zim and his wife, yes; all others, no. But even the Kid's father-in-law had been an Agency policeman. A steady ally of the whites and, years before, a tracker on the trail of Geronimo and others who resisted the inevitable.

He rode back into the mountains, avoiding the rancheria where his men had been wantonly butchered, having the Apache's aversion to camping where earth-bound spirits might be anchored around the carrion that had been men; and he rode alone, except for an Indian woman — not his wife — who had been waiting for him to show up in the mountains, in order to carry her hero-worship into practical use as his cook, comforter, sentinel, and camp-robber.

Armed with two six-shooters, a Winchester carbine, the good field glasses and an invaluable knowledge of all the land he traversed, plus his naturally-acquired and superior ability to think as a white man or an Apache, the Kid resumed his old life, only now stealth became the alternative to striking boldly as he had done when he had his little band.

Back down in Mexico the limitless sweep of land lay like a treasure chest at his disposal. He went there with his woman and lived quietly. Finding that few Mexicans knew who he was, or even suspected that he was an Apache at all, in a land of other dark hides and muddy-coloured eyes, the Kid went far afield in his travels, rarely plundering unless he needed money, then dispatching his victims deftly and hiding them securely in many a forgotten little canyon, where they lie beneath rocky cairns, undiscovered, to this very day. And also, he came to see Sonora and Chihuahua, Mexico, as ideal spots for a man to raise good horses and cattle. A land where his knowledge of Spanish made of the Apache Kid just another Indian who was quiet, circumspect, and evidently of kindred blood to the land and its ancient peoples. Here, for the first time, the idea crossed his mind, undoubtedly, that an Apache could live out his life among a race that wouldn't discriminate against a man so long as he forgot that he was an Apache. A simple thing to do, assuredly, for one of the adaptability of the Apache Kid.

But, in order to do this, the Kid would need money enough to get established. There was only one way to get this money, and only one place to get it. He broke camp and headed back toward the mountain fringe that cut off the United States from Mexico proper, still with the Apache squaw trailing along in fixed and satisfied deference.

Arizona's initial frenzy had died down somewhat. The Army was still being goaded by the publicists "back home in the States," but the cowmen, their riders, and those who were in the land to make a living had neither the need nor the time to keep alive the lurid stories that were still extant, attributing everything under the sun that was immoral, illegal or non-fattening, to the Apache Kid. But he went warily just the same, until he decided to visit San Carlos, the camp of his wife and father-in-law, and gather in the titbits of intelligence from which he would work out his future plans.

Discreetly sloughing off his companion of the past few months, the Kid went back to the home of Eskim-in-zim, bearing as always trinkets for his pretty wife and her father. Here again he heard of the elaborate ambushes set up along the border and throughout Apacheria for his apprehension, and after staying with his wife for a few days the Kid, always suspicious now, rode away again.

Knowing the Army wasn't pursuing his memory as heatedly as it had before, he struck like a whirlwind along the travelled roads, robbed several stages and two freight trains, crawling wearily through the desert sunblast with loads of ore. Gradually, as the tempo of his robberies was stepped up, so also did the old hue and cry against him. Now the cavalrymen were turned out to patrol roads that were blistering ribbons in a waterless, shimmering vastness. The Army cursed, blasphemed and raged, but they never got a glimpse of the phantom Apache.

Twice he was almost ambushed. Once, not far from Florence, Arizona, he happened to spy a stage coach and six that was obviously filled with passengers and would have made excellent pickings for a man desirous of augmenting his growing hoard of gold and silver. One thing deterred him. Following the stage at a discreet distance, on both sides of the roadway but not on it, slinking along like spinner-wolves, were seven heavily-armed civilian stockmen. Ranchers and their cowboys. The Kid had actually started down to head the stage off before he caught sight of these waylayers. Aroused instantly, he went back into the brush out of sight and allowed the stage to go by unmolested; then he sat like a graven image on his horse and stared at the slowly-riding, bleak-faced men who were trailing the vehicle.

Again, not far from Tombstone, in the southern reaches of the Territory of Arizona, en route to the Mexican border, the Kid's natural wariness kept him to the higher planes, and here again he saw the soldiers fanning out across his path, utilising every area of cover for concealment. This meant only one thing: that someone — an Apache more than likely — had seen him from a distance, noted his route and passed the information on to the Army. He swung back up country again and headed for the mountains, making two strikes against travellers as he went.

The Army patrolled the country around the Mexican border, effectively cutting the Kid off from the south, with grim tenacity. It didn't dawn on them for a long time that the wisest course they could follow then was to leave the border open, and thus provide him at least with an exit so that their own failure wouldn't be so glaringly publicised by having the Kid confined to a locality where he would be forced to raid and kill for survival on the American side, anyway.

The Kid's field glasses were his best ally now. That and his ability to tell what Seiber's scouts were up to by watching their actions. He rode hard, changing horses often, amassing a considerable fund of money, raw gold and negotiable plunder which he cached in a dozen different places. His name became once more associated with every evil deed done in Arizona, New Mexico and Old Mexico. At one time the very mention of his supposed nearness is alleged to have caused the abrupt taking off of a ranch woman, struck down with heart failure. This, of course, was also chalked up against him as though he had supernatural powers, and it was things exactly like this that amounted to two-thirds of the crimes laid to his door.

Proven depredations were aplenty, but nowhere nearly the number of crimes credited to him were his. Naturally, since this hierarchy of crimes, so-called and otherwise, grew, flourished and blossomed with the passing of time into a preposterous fabrication that stands to this day as one of the most incredibly-amazing gatherings of robberies and worse on earth, it is impossible now to extricate fact from fantasy. Couple to this the fact that the Apache Kid was never apprehended, nor were his secrets ever made public, and you have a portion of the difficulties any researcher is up against in presenting with any exactitude his life.

But the field glasses and his native shrewdness gave birth to the rumour that the San Carlos Indians were keeping him posted daily about troop movements. This was the Army's way of rationalising away their blundering series of failures to capture the fabulous Apache Kid. It couldn't have been that he was far too wily for the Apache trackers of Al Seiber. It wasn't that a lone, ignorant bronko buck could out-think the Army officers. It just simply was too preposterous to concede that this hardy Apache perennial was unconquerable; so it had to be that he had an elaborate spy system that was all encompassing. On the face of it absurd, nevertheless, in the second week of March, 1890, Captain Johnson, officer commanding troops at San Carlos, was ordered out with troops by Captain John Bullis, Indian Agent, to round up all Apaches known to sympathise with the Kid, or suspected of having furnished him with information at one time or another, or just any Indian thought likely of cooperating in any way with the renegade, or — in the final analysis — any Apache considered obnoxious in any way, and hold all those gathered against deportation arrangements.

The Kid wasn't aware of these proceedings being under way until several Apaches hunted him up and asked to be allowed to ride with him, explaining that the soldiers were going to deport all suspects, anyway, and feared they might be included.

There was nothing the young warrior could do. He listened and accepted what he heard, knowing perfectly well that his wife and her father, Eskim-in-zim, would be among the first deportees. They were, as he had known they would be, but the astounding affair didn't end there at all.

Just under a hundred Apaches were herded onto trains and sent to old Fort Union, over in New Mexico. Among those sent was Eskim-in-zim and the Kid's wife, certainly, but also exiled was Chil-chew-anna, an Arivaipa chief, and not less than sixty-five Apaches who knew the Kid only by hearsay, being natives of lands and sub-tribes of the Apache nation who had no intercourse at all with the Apache Kid or his newly-found fellow renegades.

In Chil-chew-anna's case the affair was more than contemptible. The old chief had served the Army diligently as a scout against the hostile Victorio, later against Geronimo, and also against Mangus Coloradas' band.

While the Kid grew more savage and bitter than ever over this scandalous proceeding, the affair itself had an unsuspected twist to it that ironically enough furthered the ends of the very outlaw the Army was grimly endeavouring to run down and stamp out. It caused the great indignation of all the remaining Apaches to become centred around the survival of the Apache Kid. News came more often than it ever did before. Troop movements were not secret ten minutes after the soldiers took the field, and a regular flow of contraband ammunition and guns was sped on its way under cover of dark nights, as was food and other necessities, which included carefully scouted-out locations of herds of good horses, and the gleanings of a hundred way stations where Apache hostlers watched the coming and going of travellers.

The Kid, using this information to its fullest value, rode now much as old Geronimo had in days gone by. He would come storming down out of the heights with his superbly-mounted, hard-riding reavers, cross the open desert like a whirlwind, strike wherever he found white men or Mexicans. Nor were Indians immune from his fury, now, if they were in any way suspect. Leaving the broken bodies lying in pools of blood, he would lead his men away like so many ghosts, doubling back in his tracks, deliberately crossing the Army's path, and then losing himself in the scorched canyons that he knew better than any white man and most Indians, only to come in behind the soldiers, let off a few murderous rounds, and disappear again.

But this was a new Apache Kid. An Indian steeped in savagery, no longer even bothering to differentiate between those after his scalp and those not, unless it was a few tried and true old friends — some of whom were American ranchers and cowboys — and here he conducted himself with the customary abstinence of the Robin Hood type of murderer. Only, in the case of the Apache Kid, it was simply the ancient Indian concept of loyalty, which almost all Red men had to a fault. A sincere friend could, and would, do him no harm. Uniquely, too, this held true in the case of the Americans who knew him as well as the Apaches, and, far less frequently, the Mexicans.

The tempo was stepped up again while another apex in his cycle of raiding was reached — and still the Army kept the backdoor into Mexico locked, while its other arm went flinging off willy-nilly after practically a poltergeist; one with a dark mahogany-coloured skin.

The Dragoon Mountains, the Whetstones, the Mogollons, every nook and cranny of the big country held hidden caches of food and ammunition where the renegades could refuel. The Army never did borrow this policy, but had they, the Kid's history, as well as much of the fighting history of the South-west, undoubtedly would have read differently than it does to-day.

Lieutenant Watson of the Tenth Cavalry unexpectedly walked into what was almost an ambush when he found three spent horses hobbled in a small canyon where the green feed was ankle high from seepage water farther up the hillside.

Riding almost into the canyon, Watson was restrained by his "tame" Apache scout at the last moment, retreated, and considered the place from the standpoint of an ambuscade, decided to wait for the owners of the horses, and so saved his own life and possibly the majority of the lives under his command. The Apache Kid and band was forced to outwait the Lieutenant before they dared move. Outnumbered five to one and better, they dared not show themselves until the soldiers gave it up and moved out.

After this, with Arizona seething under him and the border into Mexico still blocked, the Kid went over into New Mexico and carried the fury of his raids through the forlorn reaches of that sister Territory.

The New Mexicans arose as had the Arizonans. Posses formed and fanned out, Army detachments went into action against a foe they never saw, and the white men ran good horses nearly to death without ever getting anything more concrete than old tracks to satisfy their anger.

Going the old-time Apache raiders one better, the Kid never stopped moving. If he had rancherias at this time, no one knows of them now, and no one discovered them, then, either, and yet the money he rifled from dead men's pockets and looted from hastily-abandoned ranches, hamlets and stores must have been cached somewhere. He certainly didn't carry it with him. If for no other reason than because it was too bulky and heavy for a fast-riding raider to be burdened with.

The summer of 1890 went its scorching way

in the desert country, and so did the Kid. Half a hundred miles from Lordsburg, in New Mexico, the Apache Kid and company robbed and murdered four travellers — Spring, Riggs, Al Williams of Hachita, New Mexico, and a man named Elmer.

This brought the New Mexican temper to a fighting pitch overnight. The Kid saw a tidal wave of anger sweep over the entire Territory. If Arizona had been aroused before, this was even worse.

An offshoot of this vicious anger caused Indians not specifically vouched for to be killed on sight. Especially any Indian who looked like an Apache. Neolithic America faced this storm with mixed feelings. Some Indians spoke out furiously against the Kid and his raiders for what they were causing to happen to all Indians. Other Red men cheered him on, nurturing a fierce hope in their silent hearts that he would be the messiah all Indians were always looking for, to rid them of the despised white rulers.

But for the Kid and his pardners, there was no time for abstractions, for Captain Alex Keyes and fifteen cavalrymen, accompanied by five Indian scouts, left Lordsburg in a high lope for the scenes of butchery. For the first time the Kid had a white officer behind him who wouldn't stop for anything — almost.

CHAPTER THREE

In a report of Captain Keyes' mission made by Nan-tan Miles, the man who had taken Geronimo's surrender and said of the latter: "He is the worst Indian who ever lived," there was oblique praise for the Army and cold facts about the renegades. Keyes' men found where the Indians had ridden a short ways, then dismounted, apparently abandoning one horse — possibly wounded either by the resisting whites who were killed, or injured subsequently, maybe during flight — and the bronko bucks then headed toward the Mexican line again, afoot.

Keyes' scouts, jubilant, for this was August, a veritable blast-furnace time of year on the desert, raced after the fleeing marauders, more confident than ever, too, because there were only the tracks of two bucks. Their enthusiasm received an abrupt dampening in more ways than one when it began to rain, but more pertinently they read the signs of more Indians coming in to join the walking men. Now, also, they were on the Mexican side of the line. This didn't stop Keyes, because the old nullification treaty-of-sorts was invoked on the spot, first used against Geronimo when he fled across the invisible barrier, and Keyes' hardies loped on, but gradually the tracks of the Apaches petered out in a morass of mud that left Captain Keyes drenched, sitting on his motionless horse, cursing among the disgruntled cavalrymen he led. The Apache Kid had escaped again.

But the Kid, not too distant, watched this persevering band of soldiers and acknowledged that his retreat had been barely successful. New Mexicans were a tougher breed than Arizonans. Even the soldiers over there were more stubborn. In view of this, the Kid confined himself to a long rest with intermittent raiding trips into Mexico. Twice he routed Mexican regulars. Once in a pitched battle that grew out of an ambush the Kid had set, sprung, and then found himself facing Mexicans who didn't throw away their guns and flee after the initial burst of gunfire. This time he had nine bucks with him, but it might as well have been nine hundred, their natural rocky fortifications were so wisely chosen.

The battle raged all day, with the Mexicans refusing to leave until even their valour curdled with the long, black mantle of night coming down over the land, and all stomach for facing ferocious Apache killers in the night left them and they fell back, allowing the Kid and his band to pull out. This skirmish was pronounced a victory by the Mexicans. They had only lost seven men and four horses as opposed to the Apaches' score of indifferent staunched wounds, proven later to be negligible, which were found the following sunup, but not followed. Indian bloodstains, and nothing else.

In November the Kid struck hard at a spacious, prosperous cattle ranch owned by a "Gachupin," whose *vaqueros*, because of the national antipathy toward Spanish-born Mexican landowners, deserted the family without a fight.

The Spaniard put up a stiff battle from within his *casa*. In this he was joined by a courageous wife, an older son and two daughters. One of the girls was shot through the ear, otherwise the defence was successful. The Kid was obliged to satisfy himself with the pick of the *hacendado*'s fine-blooded horses, then his men killed a fat steer and, within sight of the house but prudently beyond rifle range, the Indians had a barbecue before they took what plunder they wanted, and left.

The following day a strong Mexican detachment of cavalry came up gingerly, made several pained sorties within plain sight of their friends at the ranch, and let it go at that. In the meantime, the Kid was riding back toward the border once more, but navigating so as to miss that little square of New Mexico that juts down into Old Mexico a ways, and in order to cross into his old stamping ground in Arizona rather than an irate, easily-ruffled and venomously persistent New Mexico.

Just south of the line, some miles below Agua Prieta, the Kid's band came upon a party of Americans prospecting that arid country. The Kid studied the situation carefully. There might be gold here. The Americans numbered six. The Kid's companion, Chiquito, was for waiting until nightfall, or at least dusk, and shooting the men from ambush as they squatted around their camp fire. The Kid — with one of those rare and inexplicable flashes that seem to crop up now and then among the worst killers — vetoed this idea, according to local Mexican legend, and insisted that the Americans' horses be drifted away during the night; then, when the prospectors went in search of them the following morning, the band would plunder the camp and seek gold. On the face of it this would have been successful only in a country where a miner could scrounge out more gold than he could carry, and only then providing that he had been successfully digging in the area for a considerable length of time.

The Indians carried out the Kid's benign plan, and were rewarded with nothing in the way of valuables at all, beyond two guns and a few hundred rounds of ammunition, one battered silver watch and tinned food. They left in vast disgust, not even bothering to go after the horses they themselves had set loose, or hunt up the miners and kill them for the money-belts they certainly wore.

Those Americans probably didn't know to their dying day that the most paradoxical turn of fate kept them swearing sulphurously as they sought horses that had strayed in the night — and that the deadly Apache Kid was behind them all the time.

Crossing the line where the Army's long vigil had been relaxed only a few months before, in December, 1890, the bronko Apaches struck into the Dragoon Mountains and rode swiftly, warily, to an old rancheria they had previously provisioned with an ample food cache. Here they rested for several days, then went down across the lower foothills in search of travellers, and chanced upon a herd of cattle drowsing in the shade, full of browse and comfortable. Mase, the Kid's close friend, threw down and shot one of the animals, a large two-year-old heifer without calf, and the Apaches made a bivouac then and there, cooking and eating as much of the meat as they could, and were in the act of wrapping up what they needed en route when the ever-present sentinel the Kid never failed to post on any eminence that commanded a view of the surrounding country, signalled down that white men were coming.

The renegades were astride in seconds, beating their way out of the little glade and into the deeper concealment of some scrubby trees and brush. There, under the Kid's direction, they hid their horses, crept back close to the clearing with their carbines, and flattened down for a wait destined to be brief.

The cowboys jogged into the clearing, possibly drawn by the single shot Mase had employed to down the beef. At any rate, there was nothing to indicate an ambush as the riders, named Jack Bridger, Robinson and Gus Hickey, rode into plain sight of the heifer's remains and reined up, staring. It was obvious, of course, that whoever had killed the animal had only very recently decamped. Sensing danger, one of the white men tugged his carbine out of the saddleboot and was in the act of lifting it — for what purpose no one was ever destined to know — when one of the hidden Apaches, undoubtedly interpreting this action to mean that the cowboy had seen one of the renegades, raised his own carbine and fired. The rider, Robinson, was struck squarely in the middle of the chest and slumped over his mount's neck, falling to earth.

Instantly the remaining riders swung their horses and raced for the cover of some boulders nearby, farther up the hill, and flung themselves down behind them. The Kid's men showed themselves then, briefly, and so the unequal battle was joined across the dead body of Robinson and a mangled beef carcass.

Hickey and Bridger aided their natural fortification bulwarks by arranging other available rocks into wings of either side that would give their legs protection, and the fight continued.

There was nothing spectacular about the affair at all. It was simply a case of men fighting for their lives on the one side, and men just as determined that they should die on the other side, but not so determined that they would take foolhardy chances to achieve their ends.

The Kid learned early that the two cowboys behind their rock revetment were first-class riflemen. This same awareness was proved often to the Americans when the Indians would fire.

The day wore on tediously for both sides, with neither able to score more than a near-miss on the other, but keeping one another well-pinned-down with dangerously accurate gunfire. The impasse came to an abrupt end when Gus Hickey's hat took off overhead like a bird with a broken wing, and this aroused such spontaneous mirth in Bridger that he roared out in laughter and rocked far back in his glee. Instantly an Apache, whose sense of humour hadn't been especially touched by the wildly-erratic flight of Hickey's hat, raised up just enough for a good shot — and fired. Bridger was struck in mid-breath. The bullet entered his forehead and carried away better than half of his head when it emerged. Hickey considered it a damned shame, but philosophically acknowledged that his friend had gone out under ideal circumstances. Laughing uproariously, and never even for a split second knowing what had struck him.

Hickey's situation had become perilous in the extreme with the passing of his last ally. It was now one against eight or nine, and every one of the Indians was a past-master at killing, either from the front or the rear. Also, there wasn't too much daylight left, and alone at night behind his rock fortification Gus Hickey might as well begin recalling the last stanza of The Cowboy's Lament.

The Apache Kid's benign streak didn't extend to this accurately shooting rider, either.

He was roiled beyond a doubt by the fact that the white men had managed to keep his entire band pinned flat to the ground with their deadly gunfire. The Indians didn't shoot any oftener than Hickey did, but neither did they give any indication of giving up the fight. The cowboy was in a situation that was building up with each lengthening shadow to be his last day on earth.

Escape ahorseback was out of the question. In their hurry to make cover, each rider had abandoned his mount on the fly. The animals were nowhere in sight. This left the ugly alternative of using legs designed and warped to straddle a saddle with, not run, but Gus Hickey had the incentive few other horsemen then living survived to re-tell.

He waited until the Apaches had fairly well defined their sanctuaries by shooting at him, then he arced shots through the brush and rocks where he knew they were, making them scrooch down flatter against the ground, arose with a wry prayer larded with hopeful profanity and started off across country like an antelope with spurs on.

The Kid saw him running, and snapped off two shots, both misses, then called out for several of his band to pursue the fleeing white man. Five Apaches, fleeter than the others, leaped up and raced away, brandishing their carbines, while the remaining Indians poured a hot fire after the swerving, speeding caricature that dipped and swooped like a buzzard gorged on the discarded mescal used in the manufacture of tizwin.

The terrain, strewn with big rocks, was favourable to Gus Hickey, and he availed himself of each boulder to give cover to his ignoble but speedy retreat. The Apaches were fast, tireless men with none of the tobacco and whisky-consuming vices of the average American cowboy, but they lacked that triumphant spark that motivated Hickey. The human need to retain a thatch of hair, and the sudden burgeoning love of a life heretofore often cursed and reviled, but suddenly projected into objective relief against a pattern of fiendish torture and death that made the ecstasy all the more vivid. In spite of its occasional drawbacks. Hickey badly wanted to live, and ran faster than any of the streaking Apaches, whether he was in top running shape or not.

Treading the more solid layers of ether inches above the barren earth, Hickey came to a seepage wash at the bottom of the incline where the dead beef lay, and here he swung southward, holding to his course until the mud became a legitimate little creek, and staying in this with the desperate acumen of a man who was fleeing for his life, the cowboy made enough noise to arouse the dead, but he left no tracks at all, so that when the Kid's renegades came to the creekbed, they had to travel slower, relying on suspicion rather than sight to follow their escaping victim. Slowed, the Indians lost precious seconds until they eventually followed the twisting, turning little creek into another jumbleland of rocky turmoil, and here, in this barren, desolate corner of a burned-out hell, Gus Hickey crouched behind a large boulder and watched his Apache enemies race past.

Hickey hoofed it to the ranch where he worked and told his story. In the meantime, though, the Apache runners had returned to where the Kid was awaiting them, listened indifferently to the derision heaped on them, went over to Robinson and Bridger, took up heavy rocks and smashed their heads to pulp — Apache custom — appropriated the dead men's guns and money, ammunition and watches, and left them for the Hall ranch riders to bury when they showed up in force the following day. The Kid's band, knowing they could no longer keep their return to Arizona a secret, hastened down into the ranching country to secure good horses, and took up the whirlwind mode of raiding and killing that had always characterised the return of the Apache Kid to Arizona Territory.

This time, though, the Army had a new wrinkle. Instead of putting half its force on the border and using the other half to patrol a desert that was the same colour — and disposition — as the men they were after, only a handful of cavalrymen were put athwart any southern trails the Kid might use for going back into Mexico, and the other patrols were sent out on the desert, while the secret weapon was a canny cordon of troopers thrown around the San Carlos Agency itself. The strategy might have worked at that, except that the Army had too few men where they needed them.

Proof of the value of this encircling formation showed up in an altogether unexpected way. Apaches were constantly slipping away from the Agency in the night. The astonished soldiers began to run into them at all hours. Here was a regular boulevard of supposedly-confined Indians that must have been doing this for a long time. The Army was appalled at this illicit traffic that had been going blithely on under their very noses for so long; then it became disagreeable when there appeared no particular willingness on the part of the Indians to stop it, and put a ban on nocturnal movements of Apaches. This seemed to stop the comings and goings all right, but actually all that it really accomplished was to make the Apaches shift their routines so that new trails into the limbo of their secret world were pioneered.

This circumstance is especially interesting when one delves into the history of the Apache Kid, because of the resurgence of Apache raiders not only in Arizona and New Mexico but south, down in Old Mexico as well. South of the border there was no reservation for these savages, nor did the Mexicans anticipate starting any, either. They still had a sub-rosa bounty system for Apaches' scalps and didn't want to see any of these villainous human wolves alive at all.

The Mexican system of ignoring the Apaches unless they were on the war path, and then fleeing before them, encouraged the Indians to seek sanctuary south of the border. Also, for many generations a goodly segment of the Apache nation had lived in Mexico. Now these Mexican Apaches took advantage of the turmoil over the line and got up raiding parties, launched against Arizona and New Mexico along with the recalcitrants within the United States' boundaries, making a thoroughly conglomerate and bewildering confusion of Indians going and coming, steeped in blood and plunder. The reappearance of the Apache Kid at this time gave the other Apaches encouragement to lay waste again, which they did with a hearty good will, and consequently, while almost every crime committed was charged up to the Apache Kid, no one, especially the befuddled Army, knew who was doing what.

The people of the Territory found violent satisfaction in scrubbing out any Indian who looked like he might be an Apache, and here again the whites were dedicated to the unique service of fighting a fire they had set themselves. Succinctly, the frontier was a dark and bloody ground. And across its arid bosom the Kid rode, making random raids at will, feeling the tenseness of the Americans, who were fearful of another Apache war that would pit all these wolves against them.

He stayed on the American side of the boundary line for several months, seeing the forces of law and order grow until hardly a mile of southern Arizona was safe for an Apache band outside of San Carlos. The best indication of this great force arrayed against him was the fact that very few replacements came out to join him now, when the others, satiated or enriched sufficiently, slunk back to the Agency, or south into Mexico again.

Cowman Jess Burk rode up onto a pinnacle of his range to look around for strayed cattle and came face to face with an Apache buck. Burk's gun cleared leather first. The Indian stood crouched, as tense as a spring, ready to sell his life for one shot, in order that the Apaches down in a little meadow below would hear the racket and flee. They were enjoying another beef barbecue. But Burk wasn't a man who would kill over one critter, his or someone else's. In this case the beef was his, but he didn't know that until later.

"What you boys doin' down there? Fillin' up on my meat?"

The Indian didn't reply. He was watching the mounted white man like a snake, beady black eyes alight with hatred and fervour.

Burk kept the cocked gun steady, but smiled and shrugged. "Well," he said, "I don't expect you're the first that's got hungry when he seen a fat critter, nor the last. If it's mine, you're welcome to it."

Gradually the Apache came out of his crouch, regarding Burk oddly. Whether he understood what the cowman had said or not didn't matter. He understood the casual shrug and the small, rueful smile readily enough.

Burk gestured with the gun down the trail. "Go on; walk ahead of me. Let's go down and eat." While the Apache was leading the way, the white man raised his head and called out loudly in Spanish who he was and that he was coming down to dine. The Apache Kid was dumbfounded. He and his cohorts watched expressionless, as Jess Burk herded the crestfallen sentinel into camp, faced the seven wooden-faced Indians and nodded affably enough at them, eyed the cooked meat and jutted his jaw toward it.

"How about one of you boys bringing me over a slab of that? I'm hungry enough to eat it all."

The silence held for a moment longer, then the Kid glanced down at the barbecued meat and back up at the cowman. "Is this one of your beeves?"

"Yup; but don't let that stop you. I ain't never denied a hungry man meat yet. Stealin' 'em's one thing, eatin' 'em's another. Help yourself."

The Kid smiled a little and made a motion toward their squatting circle. "Then get down and eat with us."

Burk was an eminently fair man, tolerant and good-natured, but he was no fool. These were Apaches, and unless he was mistaken, that spokesman with the hard look was the Apache Kid. He shook his head. "I feel a little better up here," he said dryly.

That time the Kid laughed, showing large white teeth. "No; I give you my word," he said, "that you will be as safe here as in your own home."

Burk knew men. He got down, tied his horse

and walked over where the renegades made room for him, hunkered down and began to eat. The unique coterie of diners continued with no more conversation — just the little damp sounds of hungry men — until all were filled; then Jess Burk deliberately took out his tobacco sack, twisted up a cigarette and offered the makings around. Four of the bronkos accepted, made cigarettes and lit up, looking at the white man who had so brashly come among them. Either he was a fool or a very, very brave man. They had to know which.

"Where you boys headin'?"

The Kid considered this for a long time before answering. "North, maybe," he said evasively.

Burk smiled, looking straight into the Apache's face. "Then I reckon you must be going south. Listen boys; I'm no saint, but I've got an idea who you are, and I'm telling you here and now that you're playing hell in the country."

"Who are we?" The black eyes were like wet marbles. Black onyx dipped in oil.

"The Apache Kid," Burk said with no hesitation. "That right?"

The Kid nodded. This was a brave white man. Knowing who they were, not one man in a thousand would have told the truth if asked.

"Well," Burk said into the silence, "whenever you're hungry, help yourself to beef with that brand on 'em," pointing to a segment of hide, "and at least no one'll be able to say you stole Jess Burk's beef, anyway." He got up. "My ranch's about six, seven miles on the other side of these hills. You're welcome there any time. All I ask is that you don't lead no posses or soldiers there if you're being chased."

The Kid arose, too. Each Apache renegade stood then, waiting to see from their leader's words what course of action they were to follow. Jess Burk's most dangerous moment on earth had come. He faced the Apaches like the man he was. If he felt fear, which he must have in some degree, it wasn't showing. The Kid spoke quietly.

"We don't have many friends. Among our own people there aren't many who encourage us. Among the whites there are no more than I can count on one hand. We will count you as a friend and treat you as one. Your cattle and ranch will be safe. Maybe we'll come and see you some day, maybe not, but we'll count you a friend, anyway."

Burk mounted his horse and rode away. Safely beyond Apache gun range, the Indians watched his course with curious expressions. But Jess Burk had no forked tongue. He rode straight back to his ranch, not toward any of the Army camps or villages where the news of his discovery would have made him a sensation.

The Kid raided for fresh horses, but his depredations slackened off after the meeting with Jess Burk, not out of any especial consideration for what the cowman had said, we can be sure, but because he wanted the furore to die down again.

During this interim of inactivity, his men lived well at their rancheria, and one evening, just at dusk, the Kid himself rode into Burk's ranchyard alone. The white man invited him in, but they wound up by visiting beneath a large tree where the range was visible in every direction. During their hour-long conversation, the Apache Kid told Jess Burk many things. Among them was what we now know, that the great majority of crimes laid to him he didn't commit, and couldn't have committed, either because he wasn't within hundreds of miles of where these acts transpired, or because they were not the acts of the Apache Kid by reason of his known behaviour pattern. The Kid readily admitted to Burk that he took Indian women with him when he found them handy. He didn't say — or Burk didn't, at any rate — that his wife wouldn't join him, although this was quite likely.

After that, Jess Burk and the Apache Kid became good friends. This friendship was to last for many years, although just before the Kid struck out for Mexico again — after he deemed it safe to move out — Jess Burk never saw him again. At their last meeting the Kid told Burk he would let him know that he was alive from time to time.

The Kid made it safely into the Sierra Madre Mountains with his followers, descended the far side into Mexico, and for almost a year nothing more was heard of him. At this time, the first rumours of his death began to circulate. Some said he had died of consumption, a disease that has proven especially fatal to desert Indians when introduced to them by the white man. Other stories had him dead at the hands of the Mexican Rurales, that half-bandit, half-guerilla, constabulary force then functioning under the enigmatic, ruthlessly efficient and sanguine Colonel Emilio Kosterlitzky, Russian-born son of an Army officer who deserted his Russian man-of-war in Venezuela and became in time the leader of this dreaded force of mounted bandits.

But actually, what now seems to have occupied the Kid for the time he was gone from the list of active participants in the killings and raids over the border, in America, was the establishment of that dream of a ranch he had cherished for so long, and dedicated himself to acquiring while robbing with such a liberal hand previously. Actually, what he did, specifically, is shrouded and deliberately obscured now, as it was then, by those who were closest to him. The Kid was a shrewd spender, a staunch friend and an implacable enemy. This description can pretty well be used in the case of all Apache Indians, and many others as well, but that he was very highly thought of by the Mexicans he hired to work up his ranch, and the neighbours he settled among, is fully attested. At any rate, the Americans above the line began to breathe easily again, for, while murder and worse stalked their frontier with almost daily monotony, at least the inspired and inspiring name of the Apache Kid didn't make the great mass of San Carlos Agency Indians restless and sullen now. The others, including villainous Mexicans who came often to Arizona and New Mexico on forays, were polished off gradually until only the "normal" number of killings, rapes and robberies were reported throughout the tough South-west for the year 1891.

Then a diligent Army man, Captain Johnson again, he of the Twenty-Fourth Infantry, who was agent at San Carlos — and no friend of Al Seiber's, incidentally — circulated the story that the Apache Kid had struck again. This time in May, of 1892, at a hovel about twenty miles or so from the Agency. Here the Kid was supposed to have wantonly butchered an aged Apache squaw, ravished her handsome daughter, gone south a little ways, where he shot down an old buck, robbed him of money and two good horses, then raced into the White Mountains — making this ride, mind you, with an aroused Army in the land — for the express purpose of raping another young squaw.

The Army naturally set up the hue and cry again, got to horse and went roaring after the perpetrators of at least three crimes, said to be the same man, the Apache Kid, and naturally they didn't even see his dust because, if all this at these widely-separated points *had* been the Kid, then no mortal horse or horseman could have hoped to find him. Surely he must have been riding a winged horse. It seems that there were no other criminally-inclined Indians at San Carlos or in the southwestern parts of Arizona at this time. Or bad white men either, for that matter, although not far south was Tombstone, at this time in its lurid history one of the most deadly, lawless and disreputable towns in America.

Now that the Kid was officially reinstated as outlaw number one again by the military, he began to be seen as before, all over the countryside. In August, 1892, Colonel Van Valzah reported from Deming, New Mexico, that a brace of cowboys were shot to death at the ranch of one Mr. Davenport. The killings had every earmark of Apache handiwork. Van Valzah, however, didn't any more than indicate this was the Kid's undertaking. However, Lieutenant Hornbrook, Second Cavalry, stationed at Fort Bowie, indicated that the riders had had their heads smashed in with rocks, which certainly was an unattractive Apache custom all right, and on the strength of this the military announced their belief that these killings were the work of the Kid.

Early rains escorted two detachments of cavalry from Fort Bowie and two from Camp Grant in the search for the hostiles. Another detachment was sent to patrol the border again, against the eventuality that the Kid would be running for Mexico.

Civilians took the field, too. The land was criss-crossed with posses again, and finally word came back from the border that someone had seen eight Indians crossing the line into Mexico. This from a distance, naturally, prudence being an exalted virtue under the circumstances, and also during a rainstorm that had completely obliterated all tracks — if there had ever been any — by the time reinforcements came up.

After this fiasco, the Army was raging mad and turned to vent its wrath on the only available scapegoats. The Apaches at drenched San Carlos were subjected to endless, tedious and uncomfortable questionings. The Agency was turned upside down in a search for informants who supposedly kept the Kid informed of Army movements, although on the face of it this is ridiculous. All Apaches, not just the Kid, used the high places for points of observation. It wasn't necessary for the Kid or any other Indian to have a spy system under the circumstances. In fact, the best trackers among the Indians could read a volume of information from one horse track. The Army overlooked this and went ahead with its scrounging for Apaches to persecute, and in the maze of contradiction, charges and counter-charges, the dead men at Davenport's ranch went unavenged. Chalked up as victims of the Apache Kid and let go at that.

But the Kid, like other renegades, was made conscious of the turmoil also, and took to the trail again. Exactly how, by what route, or when he left Mexico isn't known, but he showed up in Arizona again — going now on his known *modus operandi* — during the latter part of 1892.

He was recognised in what later became Cochise County, Arizona, and reported as being back in the country by several "tame" Apaches. News of this betrayal at the hands of his people enraged him. The Kid turned from molesting the white owners of the land and began to attend to a delayed matter of inspiring fear and respect among the previous rulers of Apacheria.

He rode into a camp of Apaches one evening at dusk, sat his horse until he was recognised, then ordered the Indians to bring up their best horses or he would kill every woman among them. With no alternative, his edict was obeyed. The renegades switched their saddles, swung up again and looked over the encampment. There was nothing there of much value. He then launched a scathing denunciation of all Apaches who sold out to the hated white overlords, turned and rode away. This visitation was a little longer coming to the ears of the authorities, and by the time it did the Kid had sought out and shot to death three known Apache informers who were neither scouts nor legitimate allies of the whites, but simply men who were currying favour.

After these visits the Apaches became more reluctant than ever to discuss the Apache Kid. He had made his point in the only way the Indians would accept it.

The San Carlos Apaches duly impressed, the Kid and band now rode to the White Mountain Reservation, where they struck fear into the hearts of the White Mountain Apaches by demonstrating a willingness to kill any Indian who would be denounced as an informer for the authorities — and concluding this mandate with the oath that death was just around the corner for any Indian who spoke to a white man about the Apache Kid.

During this sojourn among the White Mountain Indians, the Kid saw a young squaw that appealed to him, bade her fetch a horse and come along, which she did under the eyes of her kinsmen, and it was this girl much later who was to bring the alleged news of the Kid's final passing, which was false, but the story of a much later massacre she told of wasn't false at all.

The Kid and three others, along with the girl, rode into a camp of white men in the White Mountain Reservation area, not far from Fort Apache, near the Salt River, but the Americans, suspicious of all Indians, and especially chary of Apaches who came in the night, ordered the Kid and his band to leave. This was done, probably because there were entirely too many armed and ready white men on hand.

Going toward Morenci, Arizona, the Kid's band came across two dead Americans, obviously the victims of Indian robbers, for their heads were bashed in with rocks and their possessions were strewn around, while their guns and wallets were gone. Knowing that his own route could be plotted easily enough to put these deaths at his door, the Kid followed Eagle Creek for several hundred yards, hoping to lose his tracks that way, then swung down across the desert again, being very careful to keep a sharp watch for the soldiers who were stirring up the dust.

Two of the Kid's band waylaid a man named Jim Hale in the Tonto Basin area, and took out after Hale when their shots failed to down either the white man or his horse. Hale, like Hickey earlier, had the added incentive of self-preservation spurring both he and his horse onward. He outran the raging Apaches and lost them after a brief race.

Al Seiber's scouts were combing the uplands again, while the Army patrolled the flat country. They both found where the Kid had been. The Army, through anonymous informers, and Seiber's Indians by following trails that led to a food and ammunition cache where enough plunder was found to definitely establish the place as a rendezvous of the Kid's. The only trouble with the triumphant discovery was that neither the Kid nor any of his henchmen were found along with the rendezvous.

Seiber staked the place out, but when the Kid made for it, his hawk-vision picked out the infinitesimal signs of humanity's passing, and the renegades gave the place a wide berth, leaving its upland solitude exclusively to the Indians who waited up there for a clutch of desperadoes who never came.

The Kid and his new squaw separated from the others and evidently the purpose was — among other things — in order to use the ancient Apache ruse of leaving only a few widely-separated tracks going in half-a-dozen different directions, which would not only discourage and disgust trackers but also to lend credibility to the suspicion that these were not the renegade Apaches at all.

Going south, the Kid was pursued by a large posse of cowmen and their riders. The Americans were evidently freshly astride and eager. They had no knowledge that the specks in the distance were the Apache Kid and his woman; but, on the other hand, they didn't particularly care, either. They were apparently Indians, and each stockman had a rope on the forks of his saddle. That was enough. The Kid knew this as well as did his companion. They fled as long as their horses could take the killing chase, and finally, when their own animals were on the verge of collapse, saw that the Americans had reined up in obvious defeat; all but one rider, a man named William Beck, who set his animal in a shambling walk and held to the trail like a leech. The others disbanded, but Beck persevered.

The Kid's horse collapsed under him a short time later. He then mounted behind the squaw and kept on his way until that animal gave out; then, walking, he and the girl still travelled southward.

Beck's animal recovered his wind a little, so the cowboy put him into a long lope that brought him up fairly close to the Indians. Close enough to identify them as Apaches, anyway; then Beck's animal succumbed.

Cursing, Beck plodded doggedly behind the Kid. Once he thought he was close enough for his carbine to carry. The shot fell far short, however, and the Apache Kid topped a rise, stood on its crown and watched Beck, but the white man knew the purpose of the Indian's patience and walked on until he figured the range was likely, then stopped. The two men stood that far apart, glaring at one another, until the Kid raised his carbine and fired. The shot, like Beck's, was short of its target. The Kid and his squaw then turned their backs and stalked on southward.

The entire little drama went on like that for over half a day, then Beck knew they had crossed into Mexico somewhere along the route, and stopped beside a little spring, watching the Indians plodding on without once turning back to see where he was. The criterion of contempt. Fearing capture as an armed American on Mexican soil, Beck retreated back the way he had come, turning several times en route to watch the walking renegade and his paramour trudging down across the desert of Sonora.

The daylight waned before the Kid and his woman were lost to Beck's view, but the last he saw of them was just before the shadows deepened sufficiently to limit his perspective. They were heading toward Agua Prieta. He swore with feeling, knowing the Apaches would find horses and be astride long before he, Bill Beck, would; and he was right, too, for the Kid stole two fully-equipped animals in the late hours of the night from a hitchrail outside a cantina in Agua Prieta, mounted one, gave his squaw the other, and continued his way into Mexico, but cutting east after leaving Agua Prieta, along the foothills of the Sierra Madre, in the general direction of the village of Bavispe.

CHAPTER FOUR

As a result of the publicity of the Kid's forays, the agent at San Carlos got up a report to the Commissioner of Indian Affairs in November, 1892, giving in detail the known and alleged actions of the Apache Kid. Much of what he said was true. ". . . Furthermore, the Kid's repeated escapes from apprehension have created an impression among the younger Indian men that he is a very smart fellow, that he cannot be caught, and thus he is looked upon as a kind of hero favoured by fortune, on which account there is some danger . . ."

This account goes on to paint the blackest possible picture of the Kid, much of it merited, naturally, but also a considerable portion of the report based on Captain Johnson's surmise that the Kid was hated by the Apaches as much as he was by the white men, and the Army he so consistently made a fool of.

1892 had been a particularly active year as far as Indian raids were concerned. The Apache Kid was handy as a whipping-boy, and thus a legend of his viciousness was definitely established for all time.

Now, with the Kid's career at its peak, the Territorial Legislature, under needlings from Gila County and other areas, enacted a reward for the Kid. This came to amount to five thousand dollars, and yet, in spite of that fabulous amount of money, the Kid was never betrayed for it by the Indians supposed to hate him with a cordiality equivalent to any of their other hatreds. Significantly, too, the white men who knew the Kid and who were visited by him from time to time never tried to collect the various rewards offered for him dead or alive. Fear, in many cases, may have prompted this avoidance, but Jess Burk, to cite only one man, certainly was no coward. And so the Apache Kid still lived, buried under a ton of paper back in Arizona and throughout the South-west that countenanced every charge under the sun anyone cared to slough off on him, and blissfully unaware of any of it, at his hideout down in Sonora, Mexico.

He stayed at peace for a while again, then called in his tight little band of raiders and started back for the American side of the line. Here he ran into the first violent opposition he had ever encountered in Mexico, when he was attacked by Kosterlitzky's Rurales — or rural policemen — under the doughty Colonel Kosterlitzky himself. This battle was fought out in the Sierra Madres, south of the border, and the Kid's band was forced to fight a defensive action by the Rurales, who were out in force.

In spite of the unequalness of the affray, the much-vaunted Rurales did not close with the Apaches, but holed up and settled down to a long-drawn-out siege, knowing that in time they would win, for the Indians, caught without water and unsuspecting, were pinned down and held that way.

The word of this fight travelled up over the line into Arizona, and several American fighters came down to participate. Seeing this, the Kid knew that, if and when he escaped, he wouldn't dare strike out for Arizona now.

Utilising the blind courage of his pitiful little band, the Kid used the identical strategy he had used once before. There had been three Apaches killed. These were propped up in the rocks as though aiming their guns, used as targets and stop-gaps, while the balance of the band slipped away.

The trick worked. By the time Kosterlitzky had clambered up to where the corpses held their blind vigil, the Kid and a remnant of his band were gone again. The colonel found an engraved watch and a pistol with Sheriff Glenn Reynolds' name engraved on both among the effects of one of the dead bronko Apaches. He very gallantly ascertained that

Sheriff Reynolds had left a widow and had these mementoes of the dead lawman sent to her at Globe, Arizona.

In the meantime, the Kid had led his half-dozen raiders down into Mexico again, staying in hiding as much as possible, and while heading back toward the country around Bavispe they came across two more Americans, travellers, whom they held up and shot down. Then they hung around the corpses, knowing the Mexican authorities would have these killings investigated, and were on hand and patiently awaiting to repay the Rurales back in kind when a Mexican officer, in charge of a company of cavalrymen, loped up and began studying the dead men.

The Kid waited until the regulars were all bunched up around the corpses, then nodded. Instantly six Winchesters blew apart the desert stillness and turned the scene of indifference over the deaths of two "gringos" into an abbatoir of sobbing, screaming men fighting to get clear of the press of other equally-terrified and demoralised men, until the Apache guns had loosed another fusillade. By that time the regulars were lined out back over the road they had used in coming up, and only seventeen dead men, including the two Americans, were left to mark where they had stopped in the first place. The Kid was satisfied. Nearly six for one, in repayment for his dead raiders. He left as he had come, wraith-like and silently, vanishing down into the lower reaches of Sonora again.

But the squaw he had taken from the White Mountain Reservation had had enough. She sneaked away after the ambushing of the Mexican regulars and made her way back home. There, she told of the Kid's death — which was false, we know — and also of the murderous attack in the Sierra Madre by Kosterlitzky's Rurales, and the subsequent, just as murderous, repayment in kind when the fifteen dead Mexican soldiers were left beside the corpses of the two Americans.

She also said, at this time, that the Apache Kid had Chiquito, Mase, and some Chiricahuas with him. The Chiricahuas, most rabid and deadly of all Apaches, still infest the Sierra Madres in Mexico, as well as their own Chiricahua Mountains. Any contemporary gunman who wants to be able to say he has hunted and fought Indians need look no farther than the Chiricahuas to get his fill of both.

But the Apache Kid now learned of the big reward offered for him. He heard of it when icy-eyed Americans began drifting south into Mexico on his trail. Some of these never returned to wherever they had come from, and others stayed on in the hope of getting a clear shot at the desperado, but two things circumvented each bounty hunter who went south. One was the Apache Kid himself, always wary, doubly so now. The other was the certain and assured demise of anyone who killed him in Mexico, in his own bailiwick anyway, and tried to transport his carcass or parts thereof, back to Arizona as evidence of his death for the purpose of collecting the reward. The Kid lived on, the bounty hunters came and went, and he out-thought every last one of them. Even army officers weren't averse to trying for this small fortune, as well as peace officers, one of whom announced that he knew the Kid was in Bisbee canyon, one time, and was going after him. No one paid the least attention to this man, until he failed to turn up and was found dead, flat on his face, with a bullet in his brain. If the Kid killed this man, which isn't unlikely, but which doesn't fit too well into the pattern of his actions at this time, then it was about what the lawman deserved and certainly went out to meet.

But the reward stood until 1894, when it was withdrawn, and there never was a better rebuttal on earth to all those frontier liars who claimed they had killed the Apache Kid. Why didn't one of them come forward and claim the reward? The answer is obvious. Because not one of them *had* killed him, and knew it.

But the reward did inspire one self-seeking Apache, if no others. This buck went to Dan Williamson — in later years State Historian of Arizona — and told Dan he knew where the Kid was. If Dan would accompany the Indian, they could ambush the Kid, haul back his body and split the reward.

Dan Williamson was a product of his times. Money was hard to come by, and a renegade, especially an Apache renegade, was no better than a rabid dog, if as good. He gave the thing much thought, then decided to take the offer to Al Seiber, which he did. Seiber listened dourly, regarded the ground for a long time, then looked up and spoke.

"What Indian told you that, Dan?"

Williamson named the buck.

Seiber regarded his friend glumly. "Well, if he's the one that said it, then it must be so, but by God, Dan, that's a treacherous thing for one man to do to another."

Williamson agreed that it was, all right.

Seiber dropped his glance to the ground again. "Dan — do whatever your conscience tells you to do. You're no dammed soldier, an' you're not a lawman. If you want five thousand dollars that bad — then hop to it."

But Dan Williamson was a friend of Al Seiber's. He looked up to the massively-built frontiersman as did most of the Red and white men of his time and locale, and decided he'd much rather have Seiber's respect than the five thousand dollars. He didn't go.

The Kid came back into Arizona again, after a lightning-like strike in New Mexico, over toward Deming, and the stage roads felt his heavy hand anew. This time he robbed the roads of bullion and the passengers of gold and silver, jewellery and negotiables, but went about it like a man with a purpose, killing only when he ran into resistance, fleeing as though on a schedule, which he apparently was, after a fashion, because he would hit one coach in the morning and be fifteen miles away, cross country, awaiting another stage, in the afternoon.

Moving like a band of wild horses, never lingering except for one brief stopover at the San Carlos Agency again, the renegade's band swept up and down and across the southern section of Arizona Territory like a whirlwind.

The score of killings went up, but not like before. Now it was robbery on an unprecedented scale, with travellers forced to herd along together for mutual protection, and stage coaches the especial prey. The situation became so bad, finally, that many firms stopped sending money overland, and those that had to, such as the mines in the mountains that simply couldn't avoid hauling in regular payrolls, employed veritable armies of gunmen who were just short of being ambulatory arsenals on horseback.

Arrested by the natural precautions taken against him, the Kid led his band back into the mountains again and settled down to the usual wait that presaged a lessening of the excitement, until such time as he dared venture out for another strike against those who had what he wanted, now, and had to have.

While he was lazing, an Apache who had ridden with him often came into the rancheria with a message from Al Seiber. If the Apache Kid would surrender and put himself under Seiber's protection, Al would spend the five thousand dollars reward he could then claim in the defence of the Apache Kid.

The Kid must have wagged his head over that one. That Seiber was a brave lion of a man none could ever deny. Wounded not less than twenty-odd times in Indian fights, absolutely fearless and with the courage of a cougar, he quite obviously was very naive in other ways. Even the Apache Kid must have known that five thousand — or five hundred thousand — dollars couldn't have saved him from execution. To top this off for logic, all he had to do was recall how the Arizonans had trumped up charges once before, and made them stick, after the President of the United

States had pardoned him.

He told the messenger to go back and tell Seiber he might come and see him. But he never did, nor would any other man, regardless of colour, who was in his right mind, under those circumstances. Seiber, despite a marked limp he carried with him to the grave as a result of gunfire that day, years before, when the Kid had come in, never lost his esteem for the outlaw killer.

Mase was violently against Seiber's plan, and with good reason. Probably no Apache Indian had ever undertaken the war against the white man with as much stubborn resistance.

Mase had been one of the warriors sent into exile with Geronimo. He managed to throw himself off the train near Springfield, in Missouri, in a land he didn't even know existed, dotted over with the factories and commerce of the white man, and from there, with no compass and only a vague idea of where he was going, Mase struck out across country.

Following the railroad tracks was fine for a while, but later on this wasn't practicable; then he was strictly on his own. The trip required months of the most gruelling travel afoot, and he had to be especially careful, too, for the Army had been alerted and had, in turn, passed on its information to the civilian authorities all along Mase's route.

Even after he was back in the south-west, Mase faced death a hundred times when he crossed the lands of other Indians. His feat stands out as probably the most successful single instance of Apache resolve on record. Back in Mexico, finally, exhausted, thin and worn out, Mase sought out kinsmen among the Mexican Apaches and laid low for half a year recovering from the effects of his travail. Later, joining the Apache Kid, he was the foremost American hater in the Kid's little band, and subsequently counselled vehemently against the Kid putting himself under Al Seiber's protection.

The Kid's activities after Seiber's offer included two strikes into southern Arizona that paralysed the stageroads again. Both times he seems to have been after money more than lives. In fact, the second series of raids resulted in only one man being killed, although he was also blamed for the killing of a rider at Reno Pass by the name of Philley.

The Kid may have killed this cowboy. The only man who could say authoritatively was the dead man. But it is typical of the times that Philley's death was blamed on the Kid, and no one bothered to point out that Philley had been a rider for the Graham faction in the bloody Pleasant Valley war, and therefore it was even-up that his enemies of that episode — also men with long memories — may very well have blasted him to death over the feud he had taken an active part in earlier.

Another instance of a killing being blamed on the Kid which he may, or may not, have had a hand in, was the wanton killing of two Mexicans found with their heads bashed in, south of the border. These men were dealers in Apache scalps, which still had an illicit value at that time among some Mexican authorities. Whether the Kid — or whoever killed the men — was justified in shooting them both in the back or not is a matter of opinion, but it's a reasonably safe conclusion that the Apaches whose scalps these men had in their possession when found murdered were also fond of life.

But by now the Army had profited by its lessons over the last few years. The border was patrolled but never closed off. The desert and mountains were honeycombed with soldiers' bivouacs and Apache scouts' camp fires. The Army was putting the finishing touches on as elaborate a system of apprehending as was ever seen in the south-west. All designed to catch the Apache Kid.

Seiber's Indians were screened for their loyalty. Only the very select few were employed in this gigantic manhunt. Troops from Fort Huachuca, Camps Grant, Verde and

Thomas, as well as troopers from as far away as Deming, Lordsburg and other New Mexican stations, were put into the field. From Fort Apache and Fort Bowie, Indian scouts were recruited. The roster was very impressive; the desert was swarming with men, red and white, bristling with guns, eager for rewards, and grimly in earnest this time, to stamp out for ever the terror of the Apache Kid.

The Kid, though, watched these monumental preparations from a dozen different vantage points, and estimated their dangers to him correctly. The most certain danger was in the Apache scouts themselves. They weren't his equal, but they certainly thought like he and his men did; therefore he would have to keep sharp eyes peeled at all times. While the Army normally was content to stay down in the flat land, thus avoiding being baited into fighting, Indian style, the "tame" Apaches headed right for the hills, and there lay the Kid's peril, for he dared not go down on to the desert and face the troopers who outnumbered him fifty and a hundred to one, and with Indian scouts combing the uplands for him, he dared not stay in any of the old rancherias more than one night, either.

The situation was critical all right. The Kid knew it, and told his men. They went into the Santa Catalina Mountains, where the Santa Cruz river meandered lazily, and established a new camp. The Santa Catalinas ran roughly north and south. Here, if pressed too hard, the renegades could run for Mexico, having hardly any open country to cross before they made it over the line and into their home-mountains down in Mexico, the Sierra Madres.

Lying low, the Kid took an interest in social activities again. He encouraged a young Indian girl to join him, at this time, by the simple expedient of riding into her parents' camp one night, motioning for the girl to come along, and fixing the father with a bleak stare while he waited for the girl to saddle up. With a housekeeper again, the Kid returned to the hideout in the Santa Catalinas, listened to Mase's reports of their enemies, saw no immediate danger and, by riding hard up country toward the Mogollons, travelling only at night, the Kid led a successful raid against a large horse herd, replaced the animals the band had been using hard for the latter part of the year 1892, and went back into the Santa Catalinas again.

The Army converged on the Mogollons, sure the renegades were holed up there. They had the mountains brushed out by their Apache scouts and found nothing except signs of very ancient rancherias, probably used by Mangus' and Cochise's or Geronimo's bands years before. Stumped, the soldiers sat down to discuss the mystery of the Kid's movements, and thus missed him again when he struck south of Tucson, stopping two stages, one at daybreak, the other at dusk, in practically the same place both times, and with a large posse roaming the country at the time of the second hold-up.

The authorities incorrectly assumed, from the nature of the raid in the Mogollons, northward, and the subsequent raids down south, by Tucson, that the Kid was fleeing for Mexico again. Troops were sent scurrying south to augment those already along the border, and a blockade was set up. But the Kid had gone back into his Santa Catalinas, between the two places of his most recent depredations, and there he lay in comparative security while the white men stormed and fumed and sought for a wraith they never found.

Two episodes in the life of this youthful desperado that occurred about this time indicate his cleverness. One, when he was visiting a white rancher he knew quite well, not far from present-day Oracle, Arizona, and a large posse of cowmen and their hired riders swept into the yard seeking information concerning the Apache Kid. The Kid's friend answered the question of the possemen in the yard while the Kid himself sat slouched and apparently listless, not ten feet from the horsemen. One of the cowboys, for lack of anything else to do, dismounted and hunkered near the Kid, regarded the mahogany features for a moment in speculation, then asked if the Kid were a Mexican or an Indian.

"Indian, senor," the Kid told him gravely, "an Apache Indian."

"Apache, eh? Well — what d'you think of this damned 'Pache Kid bein' back in the country again?"

A shrug. "He comes, he goes; what difference does it make?"

"Plenty. Why, the damned varmint's went and killed a hundred or so people."

The Kid motioned toward the possemen. "Have any of these men lost brothers or friends to him?"

The cowboy looked around at the riders, puckered up his forehead in deep thought, then shook his head slowly. "No; but that don't mean nothin'. Plenty of other folks have."

"Do you know such people, yourself?"

"Not myself — but I've met folks who said they knew others who've been killed by this bandit."

The Kid flashed a wide smile. "It is that

way among the Indians, too, senor. Always there is someone who knows someone else who's heard that someone was killed by the Apache Kid. But I don't think he could kill all these people they claim. There aren't that many white people in Arizona, and if there were, he'd have to kill eight hours a day every day to do so many killings."

"Well — he's done 'em, anyway," the cowboy said stubbornly.

"Perhaps he has, senor, but with so many men hunting him — even if he didn't have a gun — he'd run over some of them with his horse. They are everywhere, these man-hunters."

The cowboy got up at a sign from the other riders, threw a long look at the Apache sitting in the shade, and turned toward his horse. "We'll get him one of these days, and it won't be long, either."

The Kid looked him squarely in the face. "I don't think you will. You have been as close to him as a man can get several times, and you've never gotten him yet; no, I don't think you ever will."

After the posse had vanished in their own dust cloud, the rancher spat, mopped under his chin with a limp handkerchief, and made a dry whistle. "That was too damned close, Kid. They're all over the country."

The Kid laughed, still watching the riders pelting over the land. "It was close, yes, but only dangerous if those men knew me by the face, which they didn't."

The danger may have provided the rancher with elastic knees, but a subsequent happening at a tribal gathering on the San Carlos Agency would have given him worse, had he been there. As it was, only Apaches were present, at least for the first few hours of the celebration.

The Kid got word of the doings while in his hideout in the Santa Catalinas. As he usually did under similar circumstances, he left the girl behind in camp with his followers, and went alone to the celebration. The affair went along smoothly enough since there was very little tizwin on hand, until he was recognised by several men who had small cause to like him. After a hasty parley, these bucks dispatched one of their number to the authorities with the information that the so-badly-wanted Apache Kid was among the celebrants.

The Army naturally was indignant at this abrupt appearance of the famous outlaw in the very midst of their wards, and practically under their very noses. They conspired with the Indian messenger to effect a trap to capture or exterminate the Kid then and there.

In effect, the Army planning in this instance

followed time-tested precedents. Surround the Indian encampment where the celebration was being held, then have the Apache scouts known to be loyal stroll in among the celebrants, single out the Kid and offer him one last chance to surrender before shooting him to death.

The cordon was thrown around the area in accordance with plan, and the scouts were sent among the people. But before the scouts showed up, late arrivals among the Apaches passed the word around that the Army was in the brush all around them. This aroused considerable uneasiness among the "tame" Apaches, quite naturally, since they had been similarly sneaked up on and massacred under identical circumstances many times before, both above and below the border.

The Indian trepidation was heightened when the scouts began infiltrating. Through all this subtlety, the Apache Kid sensed the plan of his avowed enemies and stayed away from the central points of the celebration until the Army closed its ring tightly and came in among the Indians. Then he waited until the Apaches were ordered to line up and pass in review, before both Indians and whites who knew the Kid on sight. He then held back until the Apaches had been segregated into two units — those loyal to their white lords, which included the scouts and a few select leaders; and a mass of suspect and unknown Apaches. These latter were then ordered to pass before the waiting judges.

With exquisite timing, the Kid took advantage of the moving Indians to stroll around in back of the loyalists and stand among them, slouched, old hat low, vacuous expression and all. It worked so well that even the hawk-eyed scouts, their kinsmen going toward the watching reviewers, not once turned and looked at the shadowy silhouette of a silent stalwart standing in the gloom of late evening, among them.

The Army, more disgruntled — and not a little embarrassed — than ever, retreated from the area of the celebration under the unblinking, blank stare of the Apaches, and the Kid left shortly afterwards, riding into the night on his horse, exactly as he had come in the first place.

After this spine-tingling adventure the Kid evidently laid low in his camp in the Santa Catalinas for quite a while. The old records show no indication of any more raids by he or his gang for 1892. But early in 1893, on the Mexican side of the line, things got interesting again. Not in Sonora, but over in the adjoining province of Chihuahua. Here, early in the spring of '93, an interesting, slightly-curious occurrence took place that indicates the young Apache was not without a sense of humour, which, as a matter of fact, those who knew him in the days when he was a cattle herder for a white butcher on the San Carlos Reservation, said he had in good measure. This is quite possible. Apaches weren't a grim race any more than any race was. Cruel, yes; they were raised with cruelty, with treachery and deceit all around them and in a land where brutality was first taught by nature, to the very young. But their grimness came only when the Red man's sun was setting, and from this era, when they fought fiercely and rarely smiled, comes the modern idea that Apaches were — and are — devoid of humour.

There was a very old Spanish or Mexican priest at Carrizal, Chihuahua (a spot where, some twenty-three years later, two score American soldiers would be ambushed and shot to death while General John J. Pershing was chasing Pancho Villa, the incredible Mexican guerilla leader of the 1916 revolution) who was well-liked by Mexicans and Indians, both, in his diocese. But this padre was a strong law-and-order man. A sort of militant Jesuit on the side of orthodox right. He became antipathetic toward the Apache Kid over a girl the Kid had acquired from her parents in his customary, blunt way. This girl, so the story goes, went with the renegade willingly enough, but still her parents were aggrieved and went with their trouble to the padre. The good father suggested the parents arrange a meeting between the four of them and the Apache Kid. The parents demurred, but offered to send the raider directly to the Holy Father himself, which was done. The conversation began with the padre lambasting the Kid for his bloody career, his apparently endless rote of crimes and his arrogance and lack of finesse in getting wives. There seemed, also, to be some question about these wives, too, since a Christian isn't supposed to have more than one wife at a time, generally speaking, and orthodox Catholically speaking, specifically.

The Kid weathered the assault in silence, observing Apache courtesy of never interrupting no matter what insults are offered, and sat quietly in calm composure until the good father was out of words or breath.

"Senor," he said, "I am an Indian, not a Catholic. Apaches have more than one wife. I have several. This girl is the last I expect to take. She is a replacement for one killed by soldiers. This girl came to me willingly. I did not steal her. She is mine, and I will keep her."

"No," the padre said, a dark storm in his eyes, for it was bad enough that this Apache was a terrible outlaw, but it was worse that he wasn't a Christian. "You cannot do this. The civil authorities will penalise you. They will put the Army on your trail. You are putting your life in jeopardy by persisting in this madness. You need forgiveness, absolution, many things. You should become a Christian, too, and come into the fold for a better life and an eternal hereafter, and mainly you should make this foolish girl go home."

"If I don't, padre — what then?"

"I will pray for your wayward soul — and see that the alcalde dispatches troops after you."

The Kid walked out without saying another word. If the padre had known more of the Kid's background than the fabulous rumours that he didn't believe, anyway, he might have understood the colossal contempt in the swagger of the Apache. Not knowing, and being slightly incensed at this treatment, he hustled off and lodged a complaint in the name of the girl's parents, against the Apache Kid, thus putting the alcalde in an unenviable position. In due time the soldiers were ordered out, twelve of them, hard-bitten, merciless Mexican regulars, whose morale, while never high enough to sustain them in times of ambush and panic, were mean fighters under normal conditions.

The Kid, of course, knew what was coming. He also knew that, with some exceptions, he hadn't done anything in Mexico to arouse the people like they were aroused against him in the States. And, furthermore, he didn't want to, for reasons which will be apparent shortly, if they haven't already been made plain.

But there was nothing of the martyr about any Apache, ever. Brave and fearless, they nevertheless did all within their power to keep their bodies from fatal injury's path in strife, just like any other fighters. The basic difference between Apaches of yesteryear, Americans and Mexicans, was that the Apaches would die readily enough, even by their own hands, but they would go to extreme lengths to avoid injury that wasn't fatal. The Americans, on the other hand, would incur injury or death, taking about even chances in both cases, while the Mexicans, never completely sold on their armed service at best, were disinclined to die or sustain harm in any way, if their own legs or a horse's hooves could extricate them, but mainly, they were not conditioned to fight heroically unless there was no alternative, and providing they were not ambushed, which rarely failed to happen when the Apaches went up against them.

The Kid could have retreated into Sonora, across the line from the Province of Chihuahua, but again, Sonora was homeland. If that area was stirred up against him, everything he had laboured toward for over a year would go up in smoke, literally, too, because Kosterlitzky's Rurales were already luke-warm against the raiding Indians, anyway.

And all because the Kid wanted another woman.

The Indians had a little hidden camp back in the hills. From this vantage point they watched the soldiers tracking them, using Yaqui scouts like bird dogs, ahead of them. It was a small column, but the Kid's forces were still outnumbered. He went up under some scrub trees and watched the progress of his new enemies thoughtfully. They were following tracks that the Kid hadn't bothered to hide, and they were coming directly toward him. He went back to the little encampment, in the glade where a sweet-water spring, so rare in that land, offered coolness and nourishment for the grass that was cropped close by their horses, and ordered Mase to lead the soldiers away, keeping them in sight until nightfall, then, after they bivouacked, to return.

Mase took all the renegade bucks with him, leaving only the Kid and his latest wife at the hide-away. The Kid saddled both horses, gestured for the girl to get up, which she did, then he rode up on to a little hill and watched the soldiers chase his Apaches. Noting their course, he and the girl followed leisurely all afternoon, and when the Mexicans went into camp, so did the Apache Kid and his wife. They weren't more than a quarter-mile apart as night set in. The Kid ate thoughtfully, visited with his wife for a while, then sent her back to the rendezvous astride, with orders for Mase to strike out for the Sierra hide-out over in the Sonora country.

After she had been gone some little time, the Kid left his saddled horse hobbled at the dry camp and struck out afoot for the bivouac of the Mexicans. He was a long time getting there, and many hours longer, even, getting in close enough to do his damage, crawl away again and get back to his own animal, after which he mounted up and loped easily far out on the desert, letting the strong odour of his horse's sweat carry to the Mexican camp.

It was a long wait. Dawn wasn't far off when the sound of horses loping toward him came as his reward, but it was a good reward at that. The Mexican horses, freed by the Kid when he crawled in among them the night before, then later attracted by the smell of his own animal downwind from them, came loping out to satisfy their curiosity about this strange horse smell.

Without firing a shot or being seen, the Apache Kid had single-handedly neutralised a big squad of Mexican soldiers, and the Mexicans didn't know it themselves until dawn broke; then the Kid could hear their angry, futile ripple of imprecations. But still he didn't leave. Not until the sun was high enough to show him twelve violently-furious regulars trudging back the way they had come, sweating like cattle and carrying only what they dared burden themselves with in their trek across the accursed, fiery desert that sucked moisture out of one's pores before it got fairly well started. Then the Kid went in, looted what the soldiers had left behind, took what he wanted and destroyed the rest, rounded up his new horses and struck out for Sonora. Hours later, when the Mexicans returned to their former camp-site, they were appalled at the systematic devastation that had visited the place in their absence. They swore, they howled and raged and fumed, but the Apache Kid's grim humour had triumphed. He was miles away, laden with the best guns and equipment, after having had his joke.

Over in Sonora he went back to the little ranch he had bought and stocked. The Mexican girl evidently was of a different stripe than her sisters, for she immediately took over the furnishing of the adobe house and ran the Kid's domicile in such a way as we may be sure he had never lived before. There were tables and dishes and eating implements, towels to be used and a well dug. If the Kid marvelled at her feminine arrogance as mistress of his household, he apparently gave no indication of it. He may even have enjoyed this petty dictatorship, for he never left this new wife but twice, and he always returned to her, and of the two trips he subsequently made into the United States to acquire additional funds, on only one did he pick up another girl, and that trip ended disastrously.

Establishing a ranch was a costly enterprise. The Kid learned fast how different this new way of life was, as opposed to the old way of killing to eat, killing to survive and killing for plunder. He couldn't successfully kill off debtors. As a rancher he had debts to pay and purchases to make. He shouldered the responsibilities well enough except when he ran out of money; then, naturally, he had to get more.

During this period of quiescence, the Kid's band of hostiles had drifted away from him. Under Mase and others, the renegade Apaches drifted back into the cauldron along the Arizona-Mexico border and took up the figurative hatchet again. In fact, these hostiles were still having running gunfights with American cowboys after the turn of the century. Their depredations went on up to the days of the First World War, but after that there was very little open warfare except in the far places of the primitive areas, and no one has returned from those places to tell of the deeds done in those unmarked, dark worlds of tall trees and lost distances. Over in Mexico, however, the Apaches have carried on intermittent warfare right down to our own day, much as did Geronimo and the Apache Kid. But after the Kid settled down on his place in Sonora, he never again sallied forth except as a lone-wolf raider, in spite of the fact that almost every newspaper and military report written about depredations for the next decade carried some mention of the Apache Kid, plus the fact that, since white men were still being ambushed and shot to death in the land he had terrorised for so long, the blame was usually laid at his door. This, in spite of the fact that the Kid had shown the other Indians that the only successful way for them to fight the white man any more was singly, or in such small bands that mobility was prized above strength, and therefore every Apache who manifested his hatred of the conquerors by taking to the back trails used the identical tactics the Kid had initiated and used with such singular success for so long. In view of this, crimes were blamed on the Apache Kid that there is absolutely no reason to believe he was within hundreds of miles of at the time they were committed, or later.

Still, he wasn't quite ready to call it a day yet, either. The ranch was established, true, but there had to be operating funds, too, in order for he and his Mexican wife to live comfortably until the natural increase of his horses and cattle assured him a steady, legitimate income.

He cast about for a reasonable way to repair his depleted fortune, and came to the conclusion that the *Estados Unidos*, and Arizona especially, offered the best solution, as it always had, for making a quick killing — literally as well as figuratively.

But this time it was to be different. He had caches of gold and cash in a dozen different places. He might — and would — rob again, but primarily he returned to dig up some of the riches he had buried in spots known only to himself. What induced him to turn to robbery again must have been the fact that all the rumours of his death that had drifted across the southland came to be pretty generally accepted, inasmuch as he didn't show up in Arizona or New Mexico for almost the entire year of 1893. This led the Americans to accept verbatim the stories of his death and, with a vast sigh of relief, take up their normal routines again. This included shipping money by stage-coach as well as by travelling singly again over the roadways. Too much temptation here, and that sardonic strain of humour must have longed for expression, too. It got it.

CHAPTER FIVE

Fate had decreed that the Kid's first trip back to the States was to be eminently successful. He rode abroad unrecognised, amazed at the growth and obvious wealth of the Territory since he had last been there. Leisurely, he studied the commerce of the white man, saw how invincible it was becoming, and struck first near Tombstone, where he robbed three prospectors without killing any of them, then loped on up country, following the San Pedro river until he was about parallel to Tucson, and here he cut westward into the Santa Catalinas, emerged on the far side and boldly held up a stagecoach in broad daylight, made off with the express box and what cash the passengers, driver and gun-guard had, and rode back into the Santa Catalinas again, backtracking himself, skirted the low land, headed into the mountains not far from Apache Pass, dug up some loot and ran for his ranch below the border.

Back home, the Kid rested for a little while, then, evidently impressed with the new riches up in Arizona, left home again. This was to be his last trip, whether he knew it, intended for it to be, or not.

Naturally, since the Kid's abrupt former visit, all the rumours of his demise were formally and profanely laid to rest. He was back again, and more wily than ever.

But something else was building up now, too. Edward Clark, formerly chief of the Wallapai scouts during the old Apache wars, had finally discovered who it was who had shot down his old pardner, William Diehl, in '89. The Apache Kid. Wallapai Clark was rawhide and sinew, vengeance and vindictiveness. The blood of pardners is ever thicker than that of brothers. The Kid had a real manhunter on his trail now. The kind of a man Al Seiber would have been if Al had ever taken up the Kid's trail in earnest.

Ed Clark rode over the land like a ghost. Many times he struck the Kid's trail, but never could keep it. Once, over near Oracle, in the Santa Catalinas, he stumbled on to an old Apache camp. It may have been the site the Kid used in '92. Whatever it was, Clark thought dourly, it was vacant now.

The days trickled along into months, and while the Kid was back at the old stand again, Nemesis was unfailingly tracking down every lead with the persistence of doom. The Kid didn't know that one man above all others was after him now, but he still took such precautions that no man alive could track him down. He moved quickly, changed horses often, and was as unpredictable as lightning.

Clark finally had to leave the Kid's trail long enough to earn more money to finance his enterprise. He formed a partnership with a man named Scanlon and a young Englishman named Mercer. They were going to prospect the country around the Santa Catalinas — supposed area of the legendary "Mine with the Iron Door," where Spaniards had taken fabulous amounts of almost pure gold out of the ground many years before — but first they had to get provisions. Young Mercer stayed at the camp-site while Ed Clark and Scanlon went for supplies. It was a hot March day, and Mercer, accompanied by his dog, went to the creek to take a bath. While lying there in solid comfort, his dog became uneasy, and the Englishman raised his head up to see what could be causing the animal's discomfort. At that precise second a rifle sounded from a ledge of rock on a nearby sidehill, and the slug came close enough to Mercer's face to inspire the Englishman into immediate action. His guns were in the shanty cabin some yards away. Without bothering to acquire his dignity in the way of clothing, or shield his demeanor with anything other than what he had been born with, Mercer took out for the cabin in a record-breaking dash that was unquestionably aided as much by the bullet as by the lack of hampering garments, and made it to safety just as another shot scuffed dust inches behind him.

Inside, the Englishman snatched up his own carbine and shoved it out of a notched little opening flatteringly called a "window." There, red-faced and aroused, he let off several shots at the ledge, drew answering gunshots, and settled down to a bare-backed siege which culminated much later when some other prospectors, hearing the distant shots, came loping over to investigate.

After that, the attacker must have left, for the white men went grimly up the sidehill to the ledge, found ejected brass cartridge casings and moccasin tracks but nothing else. Mercer, in a subsequent search of the area, found that his horse was gone. The animal was prized by the Englishman, who raved over its theft and was still fuming when Wallapai Clark and his pardner returned with the provisions for the camp.

Clark listened to everything that was said, made his own investigation of the area, and concluded that the attacker must have been his avowed enemy, the Apache Kid. Just how he arrived at this conclusion is unknown, but if it was a guess, it was a good one.

The pardners were sitting around a belated cooking fire the following morning when a noise outside attracted their attention. Wallapai grabbed up his carbine and, using the massive little hand-made door as a partial shield, peered out into the brilliant sunshine, grunted, swore, and turned back to the rigid men behind him.

"It's your goddam horse come home."

Mercer peeked out and saw the animal standing in the yard with a portion of a half-rotten tie-rope still looped around his neck. He went out, followed by Mercer, and beamed that the animal was back again.

"Probably got frightened at something in the night, set back on the old rope and broke loose."

Wallapai said nothing. He walked around the animal twice, fingered the tag-end of a tie-rope, squinted down at the hard earth where only the barest of tracks showed, then stared at the country around them.

"He didn't come too far a distance, either. Y'know, boys, I got an idea." He continued to study the rugged terrain. The others said nothing, waiting. "Unless I don't know an Indian, that damned buck will come back after this critter. It's their nature. A matter of pride, sort of, that when they steal a horse he stays stole."

Scanlon pursed his lips, looking balefully at the horse. "Damned if I would," he said.

"But you ain't an Indian, either," Wallapai answered back. "They set a lot of store by being good horse thieves. I'll lay you odds this Indian'll come back, and maybe tonight."

"Won't bet," Scanlon said, turning toward the shack. "An' furthermore, if he's silly enough to come back here to-night, he deserves to get shot."

"And that," Wallapai Clark said candidly, "is just what's going to happen to him if he does, too."

The Englishman shared Scanlon's scepticism, but little more was said about the affair until just before sundown, when the men gathered around for their evening meal. Then Wallapai checked his carbine, pistol and shell-belt, took up a long stake-rope, and started for the door. Mercer stopped him in mid-stride with a question.

"What're you going to do, Ed?"

"Take that critter of yours out to the clearing an' stake him on a long rope over there. Then just set me down an' wait."

Scanlon wagged his head. "Welcome to it. All you'll get is bags under your eyes."

"This is the Apache Kid, boys; I'll make

you a bet on it."

"Well," Scanlon observed dryly, "if it is, and if he's dumb enough to come slipping around here after that damned horse again, with the whole countryside hot for his body, then he's nowhere nearly as sly an hombre as I've heard he is. More'n likely it's an old toothless squaw, and she dassen't come back, either."

Mercer fidgeted. "Ed, if you shoot, for gosh sakes aim away from my horse."

Wallapai made an indignant sound and went out into the fading light of the spent day. He took Mercer's animal to a small, grassy clearing and staked the animal there, then walked to a jumble of rocks nearby and settled down.

It was a long wait. The other men went to bed, resolved that their friend was wasting his time over nothing. Wallapai thought so himself when the darkness settled down in earnest, with only a faint glow of eerie moonlight to assuage the heat-ridden earth. And the hours dragged endlessly, like leaves dropping off a big tree one at a time, until half the night-time was gone. That was when the doubts set in hard. He was still doubting when the smallest of noises came down the night to him. Just the weakest of sounds, but one that was huge in significance. The pushing of one rock over another. Not the sharp sound of a heat-baked rock cracking, or falling naturally against another rock, but the little sibilant, sullen sound of two rocks brushing over one another. The identical sound a moccasined foot would inspire in rocks when it came forward gently, feeling its way and pushing ever so softly against small rocks. No other movement would make a sound like that. Certainly no heavy-footed, booted white man would do that; only an Indian.

Wallapai flattened out and almost held his breath. The skyline was dark with a watery whiteness to it, like diluted milk. He put his head lower, caught the horizon in the direction of the sound, and waited. It was chilly, but perspiration was seeping out around his shoulder-blades in spite of the coolness. The sound came twice more. Wallapai was satisfied. All the doubts fled. He eased the carbine forward with infinite care, blinking away the gritty sleeplessness, knowing he might not even get one shot, and at best he wouldn't get more than two fast ones.

Sky-lining the area of the sounds, straining his eyes until they ached, Wallapai Clark got his reward finally. It was the barest movement on the far side of the glade where Mercer's horse was standing in somnolent indifference to the deadly drama being enacted around him. The minutes dragged again, and Clark waited. He could afford to spend the patience now, because there definitely was an Indian after the horse again. His surmise had been correct. He stood vindicated of the scorn of his pardners, whether he got the Apache or not. Then he saw two heads arise almost at the same time out of the grass, much closer to the animal this time. Puzzled that there were two Indians, Wallapai didn't wonder about it long. He cursed under his breath for the Indians were up to the stake now, worrying the rope loose, while Mercer's horse, at the first signs of not being alone, snapped awake and moved nervously when he felt tremors come up the rope to him. He got directly in front of the Indians prone in the tall grass and obscured Clark's aim.

With mounting desperation, Wallapai was on the verge of jumping up and trying for a standing shot when the horse moved away again, leaving Clark with as good a view as he'd had before. He waited no longer, but drew a careful bead on the nearest Indian, the one showing more body than the second one, and fired.

Instantly the bent figure shot into the air and crumpled without a sound. The other Apache, slightly behind the downed one, jumped to his feet and streaked it for the outer shadows. Clark aimed hurriedly at his disappearing, zig-zagging figure and squeezed off his second shot. The Indian stumbled but didn't pause, and before the white man could lever up another cartridge, the second vandal was gone.

After that there was nothing to do but wait again. Wallapai was no novice at this game. He settled down right where he was and passed the remainder of the night among the rocks, ears attuned and eyes constantly moving.

Mercer and Scanlon had heard the shooting, naturally, but neither ventured out before dawn; then Wallapai came trudging in with an unhappy expression, just as some of the same miners came riding up who were prospecting nearby and had heard Mercer's shooting days before. Scanlon studied Clark's face and nodded dourly.

"Told you so, Ed."

"Told me what?"

"That it warn't the Apache Kid."

"Hell you did," Clark disavowed indignantly. "All you said was —"

Mercer was eaten alive with curiosity. "Did you get him?"

Wallapai didn't answer right away. He looked at the Englishman and the others, leaned his carbine against the front of the shack and jerked with his head. "Come on, I'll show you."

There were seven of them following the old scout when he went back into the clearing, shuffled through the grass with his face nearly as long as the tallest tree, and stopped by the picket pin, looking down and saying nothing, letting the others come up beside him and stare in silence also.

"Good — Lord!" Mercer said. "It's a woman."

"Squaw," Scanlon added, trying to sound as though it was a very commonplace thing, the killing of Apache squaws, and thus take a little of the anguish out of it for Wallapai Clark.

"Yeah," another miner said doubtfully, trying to convince himself that an Apache was an Apache, regardless, "a damned squaw."

Clark's eyes were pensive. "It's a woman, boys. Call her a squaw if you want, but she's a woman."

"So," a massive German miner said gravely, "and they kill white women — don't they?"

Mercer alone put a word where it fitted. "You didn't know it was a woman, Ed. It was pretty dark last night."

"Yeah — an' she was hunkered over that damned stake rope like a boulder. Shapeless, boys; just her back showin'." He looked away from the corpse. "Damn it, anyway."

Mercer noted that Wallapai's first shot had

pierced the dead squaw squarely between the shoulder blades. Her heart must have been torn in two before she could blink her eyes. Dead before she jumped up, even, maybe.

Scanlon tried again, but he was no diplomat. "Was this the only one, Ed?"

"No, there was a buck with her. Look over here."

The men followed him until they saw the intermittent, dark red, almost black stains in the grass and later on the rocks. After that they forgot the dead woman in their eagerness to hunt down the wounded buck. Three men went back to get the party's horses, while Wallapai Clark and the others pushed on, scouring the earth for sign, and loping along exultantly when they found it.

By the time the horses came up and the men were mounted, Wallapai Clark's misery had turned to a savage relentlessness. He led the men through some fringes of trees, dismounting at times to follow the blood tracks, silent, deadly earnest and as cautious as an old coyote.

Scanlon observed rightly enough that, if the Apache Kid — or some Indian, anyway — was badly wounded, he might be hiding up ahead, and if so, then they couldn't be too careful. Taking fullest advantage of available cover, the hunters went on, but slower now because they were approaching a place where a mortally-wounded man could easily lie in wait in his desperate last hours and pick off those who ventured out of the trees. It took a full two hours for the miners to navigate this jumbled, sere slope, and then Mercer alone of the hunters found anything of value. It was a soiled, faded Apache headband caked with blood, and stiff. Wallapai took the thing and beamed.

"Hit the skunk in the head."

Scanlon looked on solemnly, then shook his head at the old Indian scout. "Worst place you could've hit him, Ed."

"What you mean?"

Scanlon waved an eloquent hand at the stiff rag. "He's done a heap of travellin' since you potted him, and a man hit hard in the head don't go very far — if he's bad hit."

"Another thing," an older, grizzled man with a face full of chewing tobacco said, "that I been thinkin' is that this here's not frothy blood, like you see around a man that's fatal hit, boys. If this bronko could run like that after getting clipped in the head then he ain't hit bad at all. Hell, it might've been his ear, for all we know. Leastways, if it'd been even a good crease it'd of downed him then and there. No, I'm afraid this is one horse thievin' son of a buck that's got clean away, headband or no headband."

And that prospector was right, too. The Apache Kid had gotten away. He travelled straight for old San Carlos Reservation, haunt of his youth and the intervals when he'd wanted to be free of danger for a while, and here he was hidden in the strictest secrecy for three weeks, until the ragged gash above his ear healed. Wallapai Clark always swore he had killed the Apache Kid, but others knew better. He wouldn't have had to travel far to find out otherwise, except that the two friends who hid the Kid at San Carlos would have died before they would have told anyone that the Kid's wound, while painful, wasn't even serious.

One thing, though, abetted Clark's avowal that he had downed the Kid. The Army went along with the possibility that the Kid had crawled into a cave somewhere, or into a rocky little slit in the land, and died there. Clark wanted to believe he had avenged Diehl, his old pardner, but the Army just wanted to be rid of a headache for all time, and here was the first chance they had ever had to find a way out. The Kid's name wasn't mentioned in reports any more. Newspapers took the cue, and probably for the first time in American history the law and citizenry was glad to succumb to its own hoodwinking, and bury an outlaw it simply could not cope with alive.

But the Apache Kid wasn't dead. He didn't die for decades later. In fact, he outlived almost every man who had hunted him at one time or another, and that was a large order, too, for few manhunters didn't try their luck at least once, on the trail of the elusive Apache Kid.

After his recovery the Kid heard how Clark swore he had killed him. There was no bitterness in him over the near-fatal shooting. In fact, it was amusing in an ironic sense, and had a singular advantage that worked for the Kid. Believed dead, in fact said beyond a doubt to be dead, the crowning humiliation would be to make these white men acknowledge him alive by taking up his old life again. But he didn't know the white men as well as he thought. They had said he was dead, and wouldn't reverse themselves come hell or high water. Nor did they, ever. The Apache Kid died as far as the Arizonans, New Mexicans and the Army was concerned, in the early part of 1894!

But the Kid's closest shave yet inspired him with more caution than ever. He was positively identified as the Apache who attacked Mercer in the creek and stole the Englishman's horse, then tried to re-steal the animal, through identification of the dead squaw. She was the youngest daughter of a man who admitted that the Kid had made off with her only two days before she was shot down and killed by Wallapai Clark. Thus, you have the second exploit of the Apache Kid after leaving his ranch in Sonora, and the last time he appropriated a woman, contenting himself from then on with the petty tyrant who ran his home south of the border. Women, as happens now and then, brought disaster in their wake. Even Apaches weren't immune to this mysterious scourge that finds the thorns of the rose far more formidable than the aroma is pleasing.

Back in Mexico with more of his secreted loot, enough to care for his needs for quite a while, the Kid worked his ranch until late summer of '94, then he went south into Mexico, a long way from Sonora, and quite innocently ran into the most dangerous escapade of his life. Wiser than most renegades, the Apache Kid knew when to quit. Wallapai Clark's bullet had convinced him that Arizona was passé as far as he was concerned, and Mexico, since it was his homeland, was no place to stir up animosity. But Fate decreed that he was to come closest to death south of the border. Closer even than he had come when Clark had wounded him, and innocently, too.

The incident occurred in Chihuahua, not

many miles above the Durango border. Here the Kid had scouted the country for brood mares, bought a good herd and was heading homeward with them in the company of two Mexican *vaqueros,* when the quasi-legal constabulary force of the locality he was passing through heard of this Indian who had a belt full of money strapped around his lean belly under his old shirt. At this time Mexico was a land where the best law enforcement agencies were manned by either ex-bandits or those weaning themselves away from lawlessness in order to participate legally in plundering their former brothers in arms. The law, in almost all cases, was an elastic affair subject to the immediate interpretation and expedition of the arresting or apprehending officer. Like the American West at that time, the best gunmen were corralled for law enforcement work; the only difference between renegades and bandits very often was the cloak of dubious respectability acquired from a metal badge, but the hearts beneath, in most cases, were still as black as ever.

The Kid corralled his animals in a hovel of a little town where the heat was murderous, augmented by millions of obnoxious insects that included fireflies, gnats of every description, and flies of all sizes and shapes. The Kid went to a cantina with his riders and had some drinks. While they were there a corporal of Rurales and two villainous troopers came in, looked around, spied the Kid and approached him with a bland smile. He was Antonio Lopez — as convenient a name as any — and so introduced himself, at the same time asking the Kid who he was and what he was doing.

"Buying horses, senor."

"You are a rancher, then?"

"*Si*, in Sonora."

"You are an Indian, are you not?"

"I am."

The corporal had planted the idea firmly in the minds of the Mexican denizens of the cantina that here was an Indian, lowest form of life in Mexico, who was buying horses. Unquestionably, since this was an *Indio*, he must be a robber. Certainly, since he had money to spend, he *had* to be a robber.

"And this money, senor; it is perhaps the money of some ranchero who has entrusted this horse-buying mission to you — correct?"

"Incorrect, senor. This money is mine, and so are the horses I've bought with it." The Kid's patience was wearing very thin. If he had been in Arizona now he would have shot the annoying policeman dead and taken his chances on running for it, but this was Mexico; he wanted no animosity aroused against the Apache Kid here — if it could be avoided.

The error in the Kid's understanding was just that — this *was* Mexico; thieves and killers were rampant here.

The corporal looked intently at the two Mexican *vaqueros,* who blanched under the stare, for Rurales had the power of life and death on the spot and were never called in to explain their killings, except in a very cursory way.

"And these riders, senor — they are in your employ?"

"They are, and have been since I left Sonora. Why are you so interested?"

A shrug, an insolent smile and a broad-handed gesture. "There is much horse stealing going on now. We want to be sure your horses are legally possessed by you."

The Kid's muddy eyes flicked in contempt. That wasn't it, and he knew it. It might be the horses themselves or the money around his middle which they conceivably would have heard of, these legalised bandits, but it certainly wasn't a question of legal ownership that inspired the rapacious, cold looks in those black eyes. He dug out the bills of sales and handed them to the officer. Lopez read them in the deep and abiding silence that held the cantina in its grip, folded them and shoved his balled-up fist toward a pocket. The Kid's patience was gone now. Corporal Lopez didn't know it, or he probably would have reacted much differently, but he was facing the wooden expression that prefaced whirlwind action by the dreaded Apache Kid.

"The papers, Senor Corporal, if you please."

"I'll keep them. They must be investigated. Perhaps they aren't in order. Forgeries, even."

The Kid shook his head and moved away from the bar. His two *vaqueros* sidled farther away, fear, like a moist sheathing, over their eyes.

"Senor — without those papers I have no legal record of ownership for those horses. If I am stopped later on, what can I show the Rurales to convince them my horses were properly bought and paid for?"

"Nothing," Lopez conceded glibly, "but it is not impossible, *Senor Indio*, that these horses are stolen animals in spite of the paper."

It was obvious at last that the Rurale officer had deliberately provoked the shabby Indian in front of him. The Kid knew it now. An Indian would be killed; unfortunate, but necessary. Anyway, there were many Indians. But of the most importance was that the killers would acquire a good band of select brood mares, and the swollen money-belt this Indian wore as well. A stroke of exceptionally good luck. Normally a Rurale had to kill many men to get half of what he would get here.

And yet Antonio Lopez wasn't a thoroughly unfair man, either. "Senor," he said, "a man can do worse than lose a herd of horses. He can lose his life."

There it was, the alternative. But the Kid wasn't fooled, either. If he rode away now, it would be alone. The *vaqueros,* if they hadn't deserted him already under the cold stare of the Rurale officer, would desert him as soon as he was clear of the village. After that it would be a simple matter of riding him down, shooting him to death and leaving the plundered carcass on the desert, where no one cared, anyway.

The Kid lounged back, thinking. He could say nothing. The next remark he gave would be the cue for the three soldier-policemen to either smile and rob him before fifteen witnesses who wouldn't dare admit, ever, having been present, or, if he chose to say what was in his seething mind right then, the guns of the three Rurales would leap out and cut him down. It was a moment for action, not talk. He acted.

The corporal was less than five feet in front of him, a thick-set, massively-built man, exuding sour perspiration and malevolence, waiting for the Indian to speak. Directly behind him, but a little on either side, were the two troopers, rat-faced men, weighted down with bandoliers, guns and knives.

When the Kid moved, it was with all the supple speed of the foremost Apache renegade of his time. He kicked out and doubled the corporal over; then, before anyone in the silent room could even gasp, he had tugged a pistol from under his worn old shirt and fired almost into the chest of one of the troopers. The man made a hideously high-pitched wail and fell backwards. Without the time to cock the gun again, the Kid slashed at the second Rurale and knocked the man down, but he had been moving away as the blow struck, and, while he was bowled over, he didn't lose consciousness in spite of a broken nose that sprayed blood.

The Kid didn't wait to see if his *vaqueros* were following — they weren't — as he bolted out the doorless opening into the dusty, crooked roadway beyond, sprinted to his horse, jumped aboard and raced down to the faggot corral where his brood mares were, roped the old gate, and rode off to the limit of his riata until the thing broke loose and sailed high and fell in a thick dustcloud, making such a racket that his mares broke out of the corral snorting in terror and fled wildly northward, out across the countryside, with the Kid bent low and riding like the wind behind them.

The Rurale corporal and his trooper with the smashed face went for reinforcements, leaving their dead companion to the tender mercies of the villagers, who undoubtedly vented their fear-inspired hatred for all Rurales on his inert carcass before they dragged him out beyond town and left him, carrion for the ever-present vultures that gleaned the land.

The Kid knew pursuit would be a matter of hours, perhaps less, depending on how close the nearest Rurale command post was. He held his mares to a belly-down run as long as he dared, heading for Sonora in as direct a route as he knew how. Back in the Sierra Madres he had friends. Immunity was a matter of gold there, even among other Rurales, and he had it.

But along the upper Papigotchic river the Kid was destined to lose his horses after all. The Mexican Rurales, elite of the Republic's constabulary forces, were ruled by a very able and ruthless man. Emilio Kosterlitzky had seen the American Army use its heliographs. Noting how effective this system of signalling with mirrors that reflected the sun's rays from mountain peaks was, he had made up his own codes and had his specialists trained two years before the Kid's current escapade. The full import of this signalling service was borne home to the Kid when he suddenly saw a dustcloud approaching him from the north. Reining in, he looked behind. Another dustcloud there. He recalled the American Army's use of polished steel mirrors. There could be no other explanation. The telegraph, in Mexico, wasn't out of its swaddling clothes. There was only one course open now. Day was fast failing. In the dark hours an Apache would dare where a Mexican wouldn't. He turned his band of horses toward the river, westward, and jogged toward it.

The entire affair was now in the hands of Fate. The Rurales couldn't help but see the dust banner raised by the Kid's mares, any more than he could help seeing where his enemies were converging toward him. Each watched the other. Failing light alone would hide those tell-tale, dirty streamers that arose into the humid air from under the horses' hooves, and the Kid was pushing for the river with a lean hope that he could ford it, thus placing at least the only available deterrent before the soldier-policemen, that was handy. It wasn't much, and would prove so, but there was nothing else, just the darkness, and he couldn't sit still waiting for that.

The land was vast and wild, where the Apache Kid was, when the sun sank finally. It was a place of swarming insects by night and day in the summertime, of scurrilous winds and capricious cold in the crystal clear winter days, but this was late summer, with a shimmering heatblast that made sweat run fast and glisten off the brood mares by the time the Kid was close enough to the river to see it — and also to look behind where some Indian, probably Yaqui, scouts were hanging back, motioning frantically to the Rurales that the prey was in sight.

Fate dealt her hand with maddening slowness. The shadows deepened gradually, languorously, as the Mexicans swung in behind the Kid and pushed their horses hard. The Apache could see no escape now, with his band of horses. He would have to fight for his life — and the money around his middle — now. They were indivisible, those two.

When darkness came down with its mantling, velvet obscurity, the Kid had abandoned his mares and was riding for the river alone, on the spent animal under him, wondering if this was to be his last foray; finding sardonic, coarse amusement in the fact that, if he died now, which was more than likely, he would do so defending his legitimately-purchased horses. There was much food for thought in that, but not much time to spend in reflecting. The Mexicans raised a yell and spurred toward the river-bank, where the Kid had disappeared in the gloom, but the Kid had to dismount before an ironic obstacle that he hadn't for a moment considered. A flange of earth too steep for his horse to navigate in the darkness, that led down to the river.

He threw himself down, carbine cocked, and watched the spent saddle horse amble away along the precipitous river-bank, smelling the drink he wanted so badly and couldn't get unless he discovered a way of getting down from the cliffs.

The Kid had forgotten the animal as soon as he left the saddle. He was helplessly afoot in this land, and knew it. The Mexicans were still mounted; he wasn't. If he lasted out the night, dawn would limn him unmercifully. After that a man afoot — even an Apache — couldn't stand a chance.

When the first shot came, the Kid ignored it. The Mexicans were feeling their way with bullets, angling for a reply that would pinpoint the Rurale-killing Indian. They didn't get an answer. From time to time they fired, all wild, blind shots, and the Apache Kid didn't fire once. He lay in a perfect cloud of curious insects, as angered by them as by the fierce, cautious men seeking him through the darkness. The stalemate lasted a long time; then one Rurale, more imprudent or more courageous than the others, called out:

"Come out without your guns, *Indio;* you don't stand a chance."

The Kid kept the silence. Answering would place him as quickly as firing at them would. The Mexican wouldn't give up, though.

"If you come out now, you'll be tried in a court — otherwise — no."

The Kid smiled. A Mexican military court was even more notoriously disinclined to spend much time on a prisoner than an American lynch mob. He still said nothing.

There was a long silence; then the Mexican called out to someone nearby: "I don't think he's there."

"Perhaps not," the invisible companion answered cautiously, "but one would be a fool to make certain."

"Who knows?" the first Rurale said impatiently. "He may even have drowned in the river — or floated away on a log."

The same voice conceded to those possibilities, too, but in a tone that rattled with dryness and an absolute indifference as to the Apache Kid's fate, if doubting the first man meant the second would have to investigate.

The Kid lay motionless, enjoying the squeamishness of the Rurales with grim humour.

More than an hour later, with a breathless, pregnant stillness over the desert and with hosts of blood-sucking insects making existence almost unbearable, the Kid was considering throwing himself off the river-bank, trusting to luck that the water would be deep enough to break the fall, when he heard the sound of metal on rock. Instantly he knew this would be the arrogant, impatient Rurale. Waiting with greater patience than even Wallapai Clark had used, months back, the Kid tracked each small sound with his rifle barrel; then the noises ceased altogether. The Mexican was well within rifle range; probably within pistol range, and he was a *coyote vaquero*, too, for now he was lying perfectly still, waiting for any sound at all that would tell him where the Kid was.

The antagonists seemed to be alone in the darkness, neither moving. The other Rurales had either gone back to establish a camp or, more likely, had fanned out in a large half-circle, pinning the Kid to the edge of the river, intending to hold him there until dawn, then cut him to pieces at long range. At least the Kid would have done it like that, if positions had been reversed, but they weren't, and that clever Rurale was out in front of him somewhere, gun levelled and cocked just like the Kid's gun was, positioned to enforce an impasse on the deadliest Apache Indian then alive.

The stalemate lasted through endless time that went stalking blindly, sluggishly, down the long night, and the Kid's heritage of savagery and absolutely endless self-discipline made him victorious. The Rurale apparently became more convinced than ever that he was alone by the river-bank, as the hours fell away, and moved forward again, lying flat and inching his way, using his cocked carbine as an aid to the awkward crawling gait he used.

When the Kid finally saw him it was much like it had been for Wallapai Clark. Just a hunched-up silhouette that arose and fell back with rhythmic regularity as the Mexican hitched his way toward the river-bank.

But the Mexican was aiming for a spot to the near-right of the Kid. His head came up now and then for seconds, swinging like the head of an owl, then ducked back again into the darkness just above the earth. The Kid waited doggedly, then worked his carbine up with infinite patience, making no sound, and waited. The next time the head came up the Kid caught the outline in his front sight, drew it carefully, almost caressingly down along the dull barrel of his gun to the rear sight, and squeezed the trigger with a gentle hug.

The night blew apart under the stunning explosion. Men cried out in sudden alarm and consternation, the sound of their spurs making small music as they fled precipitously for any kind of cover. But the Kid heard without heeding. He watched, fascinated, as the Rurale who had been stalking him held himself rigid for a moment, then very gently lowered his head as though overcome with weariness, and let it fall on one arm. The one holding the cocked carbine in a death grip. The Rurale died like that, with the Apache Kid's bullet directly through his head from temple to temple.

Spanish rippled breathlessly; sentences thrown out in fright that hung suspended, unfinished and unanswered, in the semi-circle around the Kid. He listened intently, placing the men by their sounds; then he started to crawl rapidly away, going along the river-bank like a crippled snake, wanting to get clear of where he had fired from, just in case. The Mexicans fired, too, but they had been caught unawares, and the Kid had only fired once. None of them knew just where that shot had come from, but they all knew now that their Indian killer was out there in the night all right enough. He hadn't floated away.

CHAPTER SIX

The Kid crawled northward, hoping to find a gap in the line of Rurales, but it was useless; the Mexicans knew now he had killed their companion. They had called out a name over and over again. The Kid knew his victim's identity as well as he knew the uselessness of trying to crawl past the aroused Rurales.

He slithered back along the river-bank looking for a spot to slide down, but in this he was successful only in finding one place where a man might make it all right, but in so doing he would stir up a veritable small scale avalanche which would be the same as announcing his purpose and whereabouts to the Mexicans.

While he was stabbing at the endless galaxy of mosquitoes, resigning himself for the time being to doing nothing, he heard the Mexican officers rattle off orders for their men to mount up. After that he listened with bated breath, daring to breathe with hope again. The flickering light of succour didn't last long, though. The Mexicans were closing their circle around him, but doing it from the backs of their mounts, thus achieving a measure of protection. He could hear them walking their horses toward him. The last hope turned to grim despair. Outnumbered fifty to one, surrounded and being hunted down as systematically as a mad wolf, the Apache Kid was finally glimpsing his own violent death.

The cordon of riders reflected angry curses as the insects found them, deserted the Kid in droves and attacked the mounted men. The Kid noticed no lessening of their numbers, though, although he did marvel briefly how the fireflies, evidently attracted from all along the river, appeared to be congregating in a tremendous horde between him and the horsemen.

It was almost blinding, the way those hundreds and thousands of little insects pumped up their intermittent glows, let them wane and blew them up again.

The riders were close enough now to hear their rein-chains rattling, and the soft sounds of their spur rowels, but the increasing cloud of fireflies was tremendous. The Kid finally was forced to move his hand before his face to breathe without drawing in the bumbling, aerodynamically mis-designed flying bugs, and then the solution came to him, inspired by the groans, curses, and loud slapping sounds coming from the Rurales. He stood up carefully, disturbing the layers of fireflies, squinting into the dazzling, crazy quilt of myriad small glows, hardly able to see three feet ahead, and listened to the riders coming.

The idea was born of necessity. The Kid trailed his carbine and stalked towards the Rurales. When he smelled the closeness of a horse, he flattened again, as tense as a coiled spring, watching the hulk loom up suddenly, barely discernible through the glowing cloud of fireflies, amble past him in the darkness, littered with infinitesimal lights, and he sprang up, swinging the carbine like a club. The horse jumped ahead when its rider grunted and slid from the saddle, but the Kid had anticipated that and had lunged for the reins fractions of a second ahead of the animal's movement. He didn't even bother to squint through the drifting cloud of insects as he swung up on the horse and turned it very slowly out of the closing line of Rurales, close to the edge of the barranca now, and rode northward again, holding the animal to a quiet walk until he felt safer than he had felt in many hours; then he kicked the horse out into a long gallop and sped out of the mysteriously and providentially-provided cloud of incandescent insects.

He rode hard for a long time and used the horse ruthlessly until just before dawn, then he made for the hills and swung down in the lee of a sycamore-lined canyon, left the horse to browse and crept half-way to the hill's summit and looked down the awakening land for signs of the Rurales.

They were there, far behind; so far behind, in fact, that they wouldn't catch him in one day, providing he could acquire another horse; and the darkness had proven an ally, too, because he could barely make out the Indian scouts coming very slowly along his back trail, and even as he watched they began to pick up speed. The Kid's trail was easy to see after daybreak. He went back down to the horse and got astride again. If the Rurales wanted to track someone, they were going to get the opportunity. This was old Al Seiber's most outstanding Apache tracker. No white man had ever tracked him down, and no Indian had ever come close enough to get a shot at him. The Mexicans were going to earn the right to catch him now. They were playing the Apache Kid's own game.

The Rurales' Indian scouts lost the trail four times that first day, but the Mexicans were emerging from the era when a man's eyes on the ground led him to his enemy. The Kid was to find this out shortly, too. Seiber's best scout had to sit on a ridge and watch the silvery, blinding flashes of the heliographers track him with unending accuracy, using fieldglasses like the ones he had taken from San Carlos once, then transmitting this into the stabbing, dazzling flashes of light that told the men on his trail where he was. Baffled for the first time in his lawless career, the Apache Kid felt a quick stab of trepidation. He could outrun the Rurales and foil their Yaqui running dogs of scouts, but the reflected rays of the sun bent to the white man's whims — that was something else.

He had an ample lead on his pursuers; there was no immediate danger there, but the finale must be exactly as he had feared it might be back there where he'd lost his brood mares. The Apache Kid run down relentlessly and forced to earth, not by trackers but by little reflecting panes of highly-polished steel no larger than a man's hand. Truly, the age of banditry on the desert, using the great distances as an aid, was vanishing.

The Kid kept his lead with no trouble at all, but he couldn't shake Kosterlitzky's bloodhounds no matter what he did. They resorted to the same expedient as he did when they needed fresh mounts. They simply took them, leaving their worn-out animals behind. The Kid longed for Mase and his other fighting men, but in a way that would make it all the harder. He had never ruled enough bucks to stand up and fight this Mexican force man to man, and now one Apache could elude the dust-caked, split-lipped, red-eyed and deadly Rurales far easier than a band of renegades could.

Still, as the Kid went northward and a little westward, he knew that somewhere ahead was finis. He couldn't shake them off his back trail and they wouldn't give it up. This was to be his final brush with the law, one way or the other, and in the frame of mind of the exhausted, driven Rurales behind him, the end they would decree would be swift, final and certain. Bad enough that he had slaughtered two of their elite membership, but worse that he should cause them this awful inconvenience; this eternal riding away from places where a man's soul might be mellowed with at least some Indian wine, if nothing better. But where the Indian led them now, there was nothing but burnt brown hills, infrequent, lonely *jacals,* deserted by the Indians at first news of the coming of the scourges of the land, the Rurales, and always that a thousand times accursed Indian up ahead — and heat — burning, shimmering, sucking the moisture out of them almost faster than their bodies could manufacture it. Always the devil's own, leeching, gouging, sapping, heat.

The Rurales came to despise the flashes of

helio light that steered them after the Kid's trail, too. Time was when a man could shrug and leave the endless torture of the summer earth with the plausible and honoured excuse that he couldn't find the trail any longer. That was all past now. There were those vindictive little flashes that forced him to keep going for ever, solicitously keeping track of his quarry and sending him directions as he rode, hating the Indian ahead with all the rancour of a madman, but reserving an equal portion of his fierce animosity for the infernal light flashes and the cool, isolated Rurales on the mountain peaks, with shade always handy, who sent them.

The Kid saw how the Mexicans straggled. He understood their weariness because he was sore with travail, too, but he couldn't stop if they wouldn't. While he rode he studied the heliographic signals and cast about for a way to neutralise them. There had to be a way other than riding to each vantage point and shooting down the men up there and taking away their little mirrors; but what was it?

As lean as a lobo wolf, burnt nearly black and sunken-eyed, the Apache Kid was riding ahead of death, and knew it. He had those solitary hours to think. The way of the transgressor is hard, but so were all South-western

Indians. They could match Nature and outdo any man, but science, even in its simplest form, threw them completely. The Kid saw the handwriting on the wall now, more than ever. He had to stay awake, like the Rurales behind him, even though he reeled in the saddle, and to do this he kept his mind occupied. Running before men who had no legitimate reason to chase him — he had killed in self-defence — he nevertheless saw the utter futility of living a life that was founded on running from men. The heliograph brought this home to him with all the force of Wallapai Clark's bullet, back in Arizona. The bullet had cured him of any further desires to raid in the States because he was smart enough to know the handwriting on the wall when he saw it. And now this heliographic pursuit forced him to acknowledge that even in backward Mexico the trail of the pursued man was an *avenida* with only one ending. A route to death over the detour of gunfire.

Resolved to leave off his old life for good and for all time, and further resolved not to travel to far places with money on his person again, wasn't enough. The Kid had to elude his persevering enemies now, before he got within a day's ride of Sonora and his ranch, or he wouldn't live to benefit from this new wisdom.

Nor did he dare lead the Rurales near the ranch in the Sierra Madres, either. Once there, description would lead to identity, and identity to merciless reprisal for the two dead soldier-policemen.

The Kid had travelled almost the entire length of the province of Chihuahua. Now the steadily angling westward as he had travelled north placed him near the mythical division between Chihuahua and Sonora. From here on he was in a country almost as familiar to him as was the land of his birth, southern Arizona, and here, too, paralleling Bavispe, he turned into the broken land on the west side of the Casas Grandes river and held to a course that would put him over the line into New Mexico, below the dread ninety-mile stretch of hell on earth known as Jornada del Muerto — the Journey of Death — a stretch of arid barrenness that was without water for man or beast and was literally paved with the bones of both, dating back beyond the days of the first Spanish explorations of the South-west.

He drew in not far from the line, hopefully. Either the deadly roadstead ahead or the American border should make his pursuers throw up the grim trek and call off the silent pursuit. Together, the inhospitable obstacles were insurmountable, and the Kid knew it. Mexican Rurales were looked upon with sharp and savage suspicion — and rightly — by all Americans of the time and place, but Fate had played him the meanest trick yet. The little helios still flashed on the Mexican side of the border, and then the Kid's heart sank. North of the line, answering flashes came and went, too. Kosterlitzky, the fugitive Russian deserter, was a white man of European extraction. The Americans credited him where they wouldn't deal with a Mexican.

El Colonel had performed the impossible. He had effected a league of two nations against the killer Apache he was after, and this, without knowing who, exactly, this bronko buck was. Nor would he ever be certain, either.

The Kid saw his plight instantly. He was caught between two forces again, but the advantage was still his. A single man is hard to find in so vast a land, although the heliographs worked overtime telling which way he had passed, but were unable to guess where he would be, later.

Now the bitter race took on a new intensity. Americans didn't cross the line because this was strictly a Mexican affair, but if they had known who the fugitive was, there can be little doubt but that they would have streaked out after him — and caught him — for the Apache Kid was reeling with exhaustion, as were his silent, sunken-faced pursuers.

The peak of his career had been reached. Death was riding just behind him now; plodding along, head down, drugged with sleeplessness in the saddle, but always just behind him. Kosterlitzky's Rurales.

The little flashes were constantly plotting his course. Good fortune was begrudgingly on the Kid's side in that no more Rurales came in ahead of him as they had back by the river; but also, Providence wasn't offering any more fireflies, either. This was a scrape the Apache Kid would have to get out of all by himself, if he was to get out at all, alive.

Not far from the village of Guzman he found a little canyon ranch where seven fat horses stood in a somnolent drowse under some trees. It was time to pick up another mount anyway. The Kid took down a faggot gate and rode toward the horses. When he was close enough to select the most likely looking prospect, his dull glance missed a humped-over figure that shared the shade with the animals, until he had dismounted, caught the animal he wanted and was in the act of saddling it, then he saw movement and turned toward it. It was a Mexican; old beyond reckoning, with the myriad wrinkles of the ancient Sierras themselves on his leathery, dried hide and the blackest of eyes watching him like a snake. The Kid stiffened, trading stares with the old one. There was no gun visible on the seated oldtimer. The Kid made no movement toward his own gun. In this case youth was the best weapon; even bone-weary, the Indian was strong.

"*Beunas dias, el Viejo.*"

The old man nodded pleasantly enough, as though the Apache Kid wasn't stealing a horse within five feet of him.

" *'Dias, Indio.*"

"I will buy this horse."

The old man shook his head. "No, he is not for sale, that one." The snaky black eyes flashed devouringly over the Kid's spent animal, flicked to the spidery, artistic Mexican brand on the animal's shoulder and went back to the Kid. "You have ridden a long way — and hard, Indio — hard."

"So?"

The Kid tugged up the cincha and fingered the bridle onto the fresh horse's head. "Yes; and with good reason."

But the old man waited in vain. The Kid added nothing to it; instead, he stood hip-shot, staring wearily down at the oldtimer. It was a pleasant spot, fragrant with shade and cured grass and baking earth. A man could fall down there and sleep for hours, days maybe, but there was the menace that haunted him always now, to remember.

"How much should I pay you for this beast, Senor?"

The black eyes lifted, rivetted themselves to the Kid's sunken, sagging features in evident thoughtfulness. "Why must it be this horse? There are others here."

"This one looks the best to me."

"*Si,* and he is, *Indio.* It won't be a good trade for me." A nod of the old head toward the Kid's used up animal. "His owner will come for him or, if he doesn't, I dare not have him in my field bearing that brand. He belongs to a powerful *gachupin;* the Rurales have hung men for much less than possessing horses wearing that brand."

"Then I'll drive him ahead of me for a ways before I leave him — and still buy this horse."

"You," the Mexican said bluntly, searching the Kid's face, "have much money then, *Senor Indio?*"

The Kid didn't laugh; he was too tired to see humour now, but the addition of "Senor" to the *Indio,* indicated a show of sudden respect that had been lacking before. He looked down stonily.

"Enough for the purchase. How much?"

The Mexican squirmed around so he was more comfortable against the base of the tree. "An old man can be forgiven his questions. It is the same with all races; the old have especial privileges." The Kid wondered, saying nothing. "*Indio* — you are very tired and worn out. So is the horse you have ridden in here — the *gachupin*'s horse. Are you then, a bandit, perhaps, loaded with the gold of some fabulous robbery?"

The Kid's smile came through on that one. Especially the way the old man had prefaced his question with a preparatory preamble so artfully phrased and humbly spoken.

"I am being hunted by the Rurales, Senor. They are less than a day's ride behind me. I have killed two of them. As to being a *bandido,* in this case, no. I resisted being robbed by these coyotes."

The breath escaped past the old man's teeth like steam. For a few seconds this homely little sound was the only noise around them at all, then the Mexican dropped his eyes and let a black glance whip over every cranny of the countryside as though searching for the Indian's pursuers, then, satisfied, they went back to the Kid's face again.

"Rurales." He said it like it was a volume of books condensed into one word. "Rurales. They are after you — and you have killed two of them. Indio — Mother of God — you aren't far from the American border. You must flee across some way."

"No, *viejo,* that way is closed also. American

patrols are guarding the line so that a flea would have trouble getting past them."

"Then you must go westward. There is the broken country of the Sierras. There are other Indians there who might help you. The dreaded Apaches. Even some renegade Yaquis."

The Kid shook his head without explaining why he didn't want to go back to the Sierras, leading Kosterlitzky's bloodhounds where the Kid would be recognised.

The old man threw up a hand. "What then?" he said plaintively. "You can't go straight up; eastward is civilisation, towns and more Rurale posts. Northwards are the *gringos,* south, behind you, are the Rurales. What then, Indio?"

"This horse," the Kid said simply, "and a suggestion to you that the balance of your little herd is hidden before the Rurales come up, or they will certainly appropriate what they need and shoot you down if you protest."

"Of course; I hadn't thought of that. They'll need fresh animals too, won't they?"

"They've been taking them all along the trail."

"They always do, the accursed murderers." Determination showed in the ancient face. "Well — I won't sell you this horse. Maybe someday he will find his way home again. He belonged to my grandson who was killed two years ago — it doesn't matter now — maybe you wouldn't use him too hard, Indio, and perhaps you might turn him loose close enough to home so he would return. Is this possible?"

"I will ride him only until I find another horse, Old Father. He'll return all right, you can depend on that." The Kid fished inside his sweat-stiff, torn and filthy shirt, grasped some gold coins from within the money belt and tossed them down in front of the old Mexican.

"It's not for the horse, then, old-timer. Buy candles with it if you wish, or just keep it. Call it a present." The muddy, bloodshot eyes roamed over the still land. "Are there any other rancheros hereabouts? Men with horses, perhaps?"

"*Si,* my son-in-law."

"Then you had better ride to him and see that he drives his horses away too. It will help me if the Rurales can't find replacements for their mounts, but mainly it will aid both you and your relative to keep your herds, if they aren't around when the brigands show up."

"And when will that be, possibly?"

"*Quien sabe?*" the Kid said. "Who knows? Tonight, late, perhaps, or during the night sometime. Maybe at dawn. I don't know."

"You have that much of a start then, Indio." Without waiting for an answer the old man pushed himself laboriously off the ground, dusted his dirty old pants, once white, ran a withered hand like a claw across a mahogany forehead, to brush aside the coarse, nearly snow-white hair, and squinted toward the mud-wattle *jacal* that was his home. "Come; it is indeed a new experience when one feeds the man who steals his horse; but everyone is hungry one time or another. A hunted man must know hunger often."

The Kid watched him amble toward the *jacal* in wooden-faced silence — then followed along. He had more than hunger within him, but the other thing that was a knotted-up muscle known as self preservation had all but crowded the other sensation out of his entrails long ago.

The *jacal* was blissfully nestled beneath a brace of listing cottonwood trees. It was a place so cool and pleasant that the urge to lie down came over him stronger than ever. The surprise at seeing a woman in the doorway stopped the Kid in his tracks. It just hadn't seemed that one as old as the Mexican man would have anything around him but his horses, a dog perhaps, and the musty silence that seems to cling and accrue to the very old. The woman was as ageless, shrivelled and beady-eyed as the man. She watched the Kid lead the horse to a cottonwood limb and make him fast.

He was turning back to face them both when the old man spoke in his rickety voice, explaining. The old woman's eyes never left the renegade's face until the explanation was over, then she shuffled inside without a word.

The old man sat on a stone bench, produced cornhusks and tobacco and very gravely worried up a cigarette, passed the equipment to the Kid and smoked in quiet thoughtfulness before he spoke.

"There is a cave not far from here, Indio — a very old place where men used to live before the Spaniards came." He stopped speaking and bent forward, using one gnarled finger to sketch a diagram in the dust at their feet, looked around to see if the Kid was watching, then straightened up and smoked again. "You could hide there for a long time. Only two or three people know where it is, now."

The Kid's keen eyes read the map carefully, then he very deliberately erased all the marks with his foot. "Is it large enough to hide the horse, too?"

"*Si.* You could manage that all right. It has hidden horses before."

The old woman brought them tortillas filled

with hot beans and flavoured with tiny red peppers. She went back and lugged an *olla* full of cool water over beside them, then disappeared into the mud house again without a word. They ate in silence, the Kid's hunger coming up from within him like a disease that couldn't be cured. The old man ate sparingly, like an old bird, and when they were finished the Apache Kid arose, drank deeply from the *olla,* turned to his host and handed out a palm full of gold. The Mexican shook his head.

"The other was enough; more than enough. We are old. There is little need for money when one is this way."

The Kid didn't answer, but he bent over and placed the coins in a small heap on the stone bench, went over, untied the horse and mounted, saw the black old eyes going over the animal as the Kid turned him, and nodded his gratitude before he rode away, in search of the cave, which proved to be something the old man must have known about, but hadn't mentioned. A hoary residence of other men since time immemorial, and the last inhabitants had undoubtedly been outlaws too, for the signs of their shod horses and spur marks were still in the dust. Here the Kid slept for three hours, awakened feeling better than he had in days, led his horse out into the afternoon sunlight, mounted again and struck out for some nearby hillocks.

He sat for a long time on the hilltop looking down toward the old Mexican's homestead, smiling softly, for like a withered, bent and warped mummy, the old man was clearly visible in the distance riding one horse and leading two others over the tracks of the Apache Kid, erasing the signs of the outlaw's passage. If the old-timer hadn't been an outlaw himself at one time, then at least he had known those who were, for the average man doesn't know how to hide a trail.

The Kid saw no flashes from the heliographs for the first time since he had escaped from the killer's cordon against the river-bank. It was worth thinking about, and he would have, too, except that the lazy, haunting dust spiral down his back trail showed distinctly in the prism-clear atmosphere. The Rurales, far worse off than he was now, were still coming. Scarecrow men on phantom horses.

There had to be an end to the chase. The Kid figured correctly that he was fresher and better mounted than any of the constabulary force now, and while the advantage lay with him again, perhaps for the last time, he must use it to stop this inhuman drama of doggedness.

Accordingly he rode slowly toward the dustcloud, watching for an arroyo or a brushy little canyon where one man could hide from fifty men while he ambushed them. The place had to have a ready exit, and when he found it, there was something else that no sane man would have hoped to find, too. A seepage spring that would smell like good water to the Rurales' horses. The perfect place to ambush men on a desert.

He gouged out a place for his hips very methodically; worried up a little bulwark of rocks and took care of the horse. Then he was ready. There was a long wait. He thought of many things, but always the perfect irony of the situation returned to bother him. The only time in his life since he had turned renegade, was he even close to being in the right, and this was the time he was closest to being exterminated. Even so, though, he felt better than he had in many days. The food and rest had done that.

The dustcloud was moving sluggishly, like the men under it, gaunt and rabid and grimly determined, weeded out now to a scant twenty-six riders, but the Kid had no way of knowing that. Even after they hove into view like sagging mummies on ridden-down horses, he still couldn't count them, nor did he try. His throat tightened. The exhilaration was there, but also there was the glaring knowledge that he might very well not ride away from this fight. Certainly not, if odds were measured up and allowed to sway the balance. But Mexicans, as he knew, were very easily put to rout in an ambush. His sole chance was to kill as many as he could and hope this would scatter the rest in terror, as usually happened. He must kill the leaders then.

The dustcloud was very close. So close if he had moved they would have seen him instantly in the expanse of silent, dead distance, when fate played her trump card. The heliographs were flashing again.

He saw them with a frozen, startled expression, and watched in fascination, knowing then, what had happened. When he had left the cave, the men on the vantage points had seen him. Now they were signalling where he was. The ambush was ruined. His desperate gamble, using the advantage of surprise, was stripped away. Now, he was cornered and flat on the ground before his fierce enemies. Now, it wouldn't be an ambush at all, but another chase. Swearing in Spanish and English, the Kid kicked up from his stony fortress, shook off the dirt and stared where the constabulary force had halted and was laboriously interpreting the light flashes — just out of rifle range.

There was just one thing to do now and

he did it. Throwing caution to the wind, the Kid leaped up and raced for the horse. He was in the saddle before a swollen-eyed Rurale happened to catch the movement out of the corner of his eye and raised a shrill, crackling sound that was pure alarm.

Racing away and twisted in the saddle, the Kid saw them yank around and spur wildly after him. Then he knew how good the horse under him was. The big animal churned up the dust and sped like a racehorse over the earth. For a while the Rurales were close enough to fire their carbines, and they did, too, like frantic devils sobbing because their own animals were too spent to close the widening gap.

The bullets weren't close to the desperado until just before he cleared out of range, then the watering-eyed men behind were concentrating on his horse, trying to bring down the animal that was bearing away the man they had sacrificed so much for.

The Kid didn't return the fire. He hunched over and urged the beast on with guttural Apache words, not praying but hoping with all the force of his soul that no slug would find the horse — nor did it, for Destiny had always her sardonicism to cater for. When the spent slug found lodging, it was in the flesh of the Apache Kid's thigh, on the left side of the rider's bent body where the skin was drawn tight, and missing the cantle of the saddle by bare inches. The wound hurt instantly but the force of the ball was nearly spent when it penetrated. The Kid ran a hand over his upper leg, feeling the sticky blood and probing for the wound, but when he looked around it was at the men falling behind him first, and at the gash second. Then he saw that the thing wasn't really dangerous, barring infection, but it would be inconvenient to a man whose body must be constantly strained during his flight. There would be no chance for the thing to heal until he was safely home, and in the meantime it would bleed and grow feverish.

The Kid's cold fury was in his face like a dark storm passing when he dared to rein down to a walk, knowing the pursuers were at least two miles behind, beating along horses that staggered.

And the final trump card was the damnable flashing signals again. Dancing in excitement, making stabs of light that were merciless and more deadly to the Apache Kid than the guns of the men behind him, because now he was closed off and could move only in one direction. Toward Sonora. Toward the matronly Sierra Madres. Homeward — the exact direction he hadn't wanted to take. And those helios were plotting his course like fireflies, driving him to earth.

The situation was almost without hope now, for he had topped a little rise in time to see the seven hard riding *vaqueros* coming down toward him in an angling run from the northwest. These weren't Rurales, but there could be no doubt that they had been hastily recruited from some great rancho to aid in exterminating the Indian killer.

The wound irritated him constantly now, too, but it did something that normally a wound doesn't do. Instead of sapping him, making him passive with resignation and sick with the suffering of injury, it fanned the coals of his ire. The Apache Kid drew off the trail of the men in front of him like a maddened wolf, dismounted, led the horse out of danger and returned to an erosion gully where he disdained hiding, stood upright with the cocked carbine and waited, his eyes bloodshot and glistening with terrible fury.

When the *vaqueros* topped a ridge and loped easily down the near side of it, not one of them saw the motionless Indian who stood in plain sight not more than six hundred feet away, crouched a little, favouring one leg, his headband dark and stiff with filth and sweat, his face burnt nearly black and his rawhide torso shiny with natural oil.

The Kid picked out a thick, squatty rider with a ferocious moustache, an immense *panza* that hung out over his belt like the bloat, and fired. The Mexican turned almost a perfect cartwheel when his horse shied out from under him at the gun thunder; he lay flat where he fell, not hearing the shrill, abrupt cries from his companions or the gunfire from the Indian.

The Kid's second shot brought down a horse, his third killed a running man, afoot and panicked, the fourth shot had to go out after the men, for they had split up like raindrops in a high wind, broken and scattered in pure terror.

The Kid went back and mounted his animal, kneed it around like an avenging angel, reloading as he rode, and went after the *vaqueros* in a whirlwind charge that brought him close enough to kill another man in the face of a flurry of pistol shots. After that the Mexican cowboys fled like the wind, riding crazily with no thought of hunting up the Rurales they had been told would meet them, driven by only one fixed thought. Get clear of the rabid, murderous Indian behind them.

The Kid reined back westward when there was no further use in chasing the men who had come so gaily overland to kill him. He was riding now with the carbine loaded again and lying flat across his lap. Escape appeared to be a whimsical thing that taunted and tempted at the same time. He ignored it in his black rage and sat motionless watching ten Rurales — all that still pursued him — coming blindly along his back trail.

The odds were about what an Apache was accustomed to. He turned in bleak acceptance and struck out for Sonora and the ranch now. The canniness was gone. All the desire to foil the trackers was abated into nothing; just the terrible anger existed in him. It was equally divided between the Rurales and the frantic signals that increased as he loped back into a desert country where humanity held the primeval earth in constant subjugation.

The Rurales got fresh horses, some food and wine, and were astride again when the Kid, still riding the horse he had taken from the old Mexican, saw them stringing out behind him. The rage had become a solid gorge of hatred and sullenness. He went westward, driven like an unwilling mustang toward succour and revelation, hating every foot of the way because of what was certainly ahead. Kosterlitzky's men would find out who they had been after within another few days. Then the last island of hope in a hemisphere turned against the Apache Kid, would be denied to him. The scope of his existence would be narrowed to a few mountainous trails and a constant changing of old rancherias in a hostile world. The closer he got to the little ranch, the more his resentment mounted until he would go no further. Better to die still unknown, than to die later known and hunted to earth as the fabulous, notorious Apache Kid.

He made his stand in a brush hedge where the pines were like needles and the only shade was low, around the gnarled stumps of ancient brush growths. Where an Indian could die fittingly, if needs be, and where Apaches had always fought frontal battles the best, utilising the accursed scrub sedge for protection the way nature had meant for it to be used.

The Rurales were walking their horses when they came into view. The late afternoon sun had lightened the burden of brilliance and heat until a requiem, soft daylight hung over the last stand of the Apache Kid with a cloak of benedictine benevolence.

The Mexicans were riding into the sun with their great hats slanted forward to shield sore eyes that raked the land for movement with unwilling, jerky movements. There was a killing determination in those ten sets of eyes. All the weaker men had long since fallen out of the race for death. Those that remained were strong with the blood of the ancient warrior races of Mexico coursing sluggishly, stubbornly, in them. These ten men were ruthless in all things, the Kid could see it plainly enough. They had killed horses in the chase and scorned the dehydrated, weak flesh that collapsed under them. They had walked on raw, bleeding feet until they could find other horses. They had curled lips in contempt at the lesser men who had been weeded out, given up and gone to earth in this mad hunt. They would kill themselves for a veritable devil of an Indian. They could be stopped, yes, but only by a bullet, these ten phantom horsemen who came into sight riding slowly, but they could not be turned back. These were the type of men Emil Kosterlitzky had seen in Mexico and had used as the core and nucleus of his dreaded Rurales. The Kid watched them coming toward him and measured each rider. This would be no ambush that would break like the hard clay of an *olla* when he fired into it, scattering the pieces to the four winds. This was to be a fight from the first shot to the last.

One tiger against ten lions.

The Kid pulled out his handgun, cocked it and laid it on an outcropping of wind-whittled clay, then he waited for one of the horsemen to see him. It was a long moment freighted with misgivings. Burdened with the recurrent, childish hopes that, if he lay down out of sight, they all would ride dumbly by him, functioning as they were, by instinct alone. But he knew better. If he let them go, what of it? They would see where they had run out of tracks and come back. Failing that, the helios would waggle their old woman's garrulousness, demanding, insistent and whining in dazzling silence. Those steel reflectors were the Kid's real enemy. He knew it, watching the Mexicans come almost abreast of him and picking them out for targets. Seeing in each warrior of the snake and the eagle an enemy despised since time began by his people.

Selecting with the care of an executioner the lightest complexioned of the ten men and knowing this one was at least preponderately of the merciless Spanish blood. Then taking the next man, swart and greasy and terribly cruel looking, and the next, stamped out of the same mould as the second man, and seeing each one after that distinguishable from the others only by his dress. All wearing the same awful expression, as though a stink of death was in their nostrils. An Apache knew how this could be. Usen gave the honour of smelling death to his people often. Usen was the Apache God. The Apache Kid was his foremost son, even yet, while he stood as though struck from one lean, solid piece of dirty, unalloyed copper — waiting.

The Rurale with the light reddish tint to his pale skin. He of the Proud Blood, saw the Kid first. With the peculiar, speculative calm of the dominant race, he reined up calmly, staring at the sinew and whipcord frame that was death's own human form, for him, and let the air jet out of his hooked, high arched nose, against slightly flared and compressed nostrils, without saying a word. He didn't have to. The others, with their cloying scent of doom stronger now, raised sunken, fanatical eyes and saw the Indian too, where he stood, legs braced wide, bent just a little, cocked carbine at his shoulder.

CHAPTER SEVEN

The Kid fired into the face of the Spanish-Mexican, knowing with the miraculous telepathy of the best fighting men that his timing was perfect. The Rurale went slowly sideways until he was on the ground, but he wasn't killed. He should have died gracefully. Instead he coughed an order and felt with numb fingers for the gun in his belt. The Kid didn't fire into his prone, helpless body again. There was no need. When the immense, consuming determination was bled out a little, enough for ennui to set in, the Spaniard would die. He did die, in fact, still with the fixed, black stare, hanging on the firing Apache renegade, not knowing that he had achieved a certain distinction, a certain elan, as it were. Killed by the Apache Kid, the single warrior who had reduced two large American territories to near panic.

The Kid's lips were wrenched into a thin line of defiance, but his second and third shots were near misses because the Rurales, for all their complete fatigue, were moving with fluid desperation now, throwing themselves off the horses on the far side. The Kid swore a singeing oath in English and groped for his six-gun. He killed two horses with two shots. That left a brace of Rurales without upright protection. One of them absorbed a slug into his head before he could drop behind the quivering carcass of his horse, and the other was spun sideways by a shot that ploughed into his side. Lying prone, all the fight drained out of him, that second man fought with clawed-up fingers to scramble back behind his horse. His terror was unwarranted. The Kid ignored him as he had the dead Spaniard.

The other Mexicans were scattered now and shouting bursts of talk to one another in hoarsely staccato voices. The Kid dropped behind the eroded little ledge where he had earlier put his pistol. The first advantage was past and spent, but it had been more bountiful than he had dared expect. Two dead, one incapacitated. Seven to one; practically even odds. Maybe, after all . . .

Then the Mexicans opened up. The little ledge of his forlorn fortress began to fly apart with appalling rapidity. It wasn't like rock. The clay went asunder in large pieces. He swivelled his head with a frantic need, saw a better spot feet away, and jumped up and ran for it. The second Mexican bullet to take effect struck him below the knee, off to one side, and blew a pathway through the flesh of his skinny leg. This one went numb almost at once, and didn't pain him for half an hour; then the mortified flesh began to hurt with increasing insistence, but he was safe behind a sedge of old copse and a miniature barranca of adobe baked into its twisted, malformed ugliness by the heat of milleniums.

The Mexican gunfire was a throaty chorus for a while, then it died away to intermittent, vindictive, exploratory shots that the Apache Kid didn't bother to answer at all, as was his way, until he got a target worth risking the precious ammunition on.

He got his best sighting of the late afternoon when a careless Rurale let one leg show from behind a dead horse. The Kid took a long aim before he fired. The Mexican let out a howl of agony that evidently had an unnerving effect on his fellows, for the next burst of gunfire was more erratic than any before, also more revealing. The Kid noted three gun positions and fired methodically at each one, with no rewarding good fortune as far as he could tell.

The daylight waned begrudgingly, as though nature was loath to leave this interestingly-unequal battle. The Kid waited for dusk with his old patience. The night is ever the ally of those oppressed or of those beyond the law.

He had come to know it as both friend and enemy, each condition dictating its fickle alliance, but this night he knew well that it was his friend now as it had been before. He also knew something else. The Apache Kid couldn't stay where he was much longer. The helios would be sending their frantic messages as long as a shaft of light remained to reflect from them. There would be other Rurales coming after him.

But his end had been achieved, whether he knew it then or not, for the Spanish-Mexican was forever still, as was another Rurale, and there were others wounded. There might be seven left to continue the chase, but at least one would have to stay behind with the wounded. That meant six Rurales against the Apache Kid, and those six would be demoralised now; might not even follow him.

He stayed where he was until the full darkness came down the land in giant steps, sweeping away the hiding little islands of daylight and painting with broad strokes the solid colours of darkness. Then he got up cautiously, ground back the grunt from his twice-wounded leg, and hobbled for the big horse again. Mounting was reduced to a muscular vault that slammed him into the saddle and tore the ragged, purple flesh of his wounded thigh so that cascades of vermilion ran anew.

Staunching the blood irritably, the Kid struck out in a straight line for the Sierras and home.

He harvested pleasure from the last battle with his mentors, seeing once more the Spanish-Mexican's odd, courageous look when they had first crossed glances, and seeing the same face moments later when the Kid's ball had struck the man down.

He rode throughout the night at a painful walk that kept the working tag ends of his flesh grinding together with small, moist sounds. There was no fever except in the wounded areas themselves, but there was a peculiar lightheadedness that made him see Will Diehl's face, and Holmes' intent, small-eyed stare, and the Sheriff's death mask, each bobbing along just in front of him as he went into the black west, until he felt obliged to acknowledge their mute looks of wooden recognition of the man who had seen them killed in each case.

The Kid spoke to them in English, in easily understood frontier patois, explaining just why each had died, reciting the long list of the white man's crimes against he and his people, reasoning with them until the night was half gone and a warning coolness touched over the places where he rode, telling of a daylight soon to come and reveal him to the little helios again. Then he launched into an explanation of why he would never go out on another raid. All these things he remembered clearly later, although at the time he must have been delirious, and by the weakest of pre-dawn light, he could tell what part of Sonora he was in with no trouble at all.

He even headed for a *bosque* of stunted trees that he knew had a spring close by, and dismounted there before day fully broke, and tied his horse among the little trees and loosened the cincha, before he shuffled stupidly to where the soft, damp mud was, and threw himself down.

The most unique factor of this episode was that the Kid had found a way to outwit the persistent heliographs without being fully in command of his mental faculties, for he knew nothing after he lay down in the cool mud until late in the afternoon, when he awoke with a gargantuan thirst, and slaked it over a long period with gulps of the spring water, lying still, letting the damp soil suck out the fever in his swollen leg, unable to move about if the desire had been in him, which it wasn't.

He spent that day at the spring drinking water and sinking into deep lethargies that may have been sleep, for he had been without it for days, except for a few stolen hours back in the Chihuahua cave.

The second night was pretty much like the

first, and the second day witnessed pangs of hunger which hadn't bothered him the day before. Also, his horse being fretful under the stimulating smell of water he longed for and couldn't reach, the Kid dragged himself over to the trees and let the beast loose, lay back and watched it drink until the belly hide was as taut as a drum, then fall to browsing on the meagre grass in the little glade, wondering if he dared try and get food for himself.

The third night was more than half spent when the Kid washed both wounds at the spring, picking away the clotted mud and blood, cleansing the angry flesh and poking it for infectious matter that didn't show up, before he tried to stand upright, using a sapling as an aid and biting back the spasms of pain that flamed outward from the hurt parts, racking his body with almost overwhelming agony. Erect and holding to the little tree, waiting for the spirals that converged just behind his eyeballs to subside, the Kid plumbed the depths of his weakness. Wondered if, after all, he was too weak to get back to his ranch, rejected the thought with Apache impatience and stood in gloomy silence for almost an hour before he tried out the leg.

By the time he could walk, the bark of the little tree was worn smooth from his sweaty palm, but he triumphed and shook away the droplets of perspiration that built up and ran under his salt-stiff, ragged, grimy clothing, making the money-belt clammy with a drench sogginess.

Forgotten places in the great Southwest are festooned with the bleached bones of men who, like the Apache Kid, crawled into natural cathedrals to die, and died. The Kid came close to joining their forgotten, unknown and unsung ranks, but not quite. His will to live was stronger, or his body harder. At any rate he survived, fought his grim battle with death in a pocket of tree studded, spring fed earth that was nearly at the heart of a land being combed for the mysterious renegade who had disappeared, by Kosterlitzky's avengers.

Five days later he rode back out into the blast furnace atmosphere of the desert again. Leaner even, and almost as weak as when he had ridden in. Still with dark blood staining his skin where the big horse's movements worried at the healing wounds, but alive and ready to resume his fight for existence, travelling on guts more than health, motivated by an unconquerably defiant spirit more than the will to do, but alive anyway.

And now it struck him that the helios were sheathed in absolute blindness. The flashes were no longer spinning out from the high places tracking him from miles away. The understanding came suddenly and he cursed. He could have eluded them days before. Probably could have gotten away from the Rurales without ever being wounded in the first place. Could certainly have lost the pursuit in the cave back by the old man's ranch in Chihuahua. Of all the country he had ridden over so far, that cave and the dell he had just vacated were the most natural hideouts he had seen, and that had been all he had needed to silence the persistent little reflectors right from the start.

They couldn't track him in the night, those helios, only during the day, and like a fool he hadn't reasoned it out. Travelling only by night, using his own heritage and training as a tracker to hide his tracks, he could outwit not only the Rurales but the heliographs as well. He turned back and rode down to the spring again, dismounted painfully and grunted. A man in flight for his life always makes at least one mistake that can — and often does — cost him his life. The Apache Kid had come within a fever of being his own doomsman.

He sat down in the shade and thought it out. He could hide his tracks easily enough by staying in the rocky land. He could outwit the nemesis-like reflectors by riding in the dark, when neither the men on the hill tops could see him, or flash out their signals either. He swore to himself again and made an irritated, brusque motion with his head.

After that he waited for nightfall with rising hope. By the time he mounted the big horse again, his spirits were higher than they had been ever before. The cool night shut him up in a purple vacuum that was all his own. A domain of rich softness where an Indian fugitive on a sleek horse rode in almost exclusive silence, making wide detours around slumbering little villages and past bivouacs of sulky-eyed, venomous and thoroughly defeated Rurales who had been riding endless miles over a baked land for tracks that never materialised, or the vision of an Indian on a fast horse that was fading into the limbo of things once seen by a few men, destined never to be seen again by those who came later.

The Kid ate his fill only once, during the entire pursuit from Chihuahua. That was at the ranch of a one-eyed Mexican not far from a mud-wattle village in Sonora. Here he dared to stop when he saw horses in a fenced field that had the different, blunt and outstanding brands of many American ranches on their hips, shoulders and ribs. Here would be a Mexican who lived by either robbery or in league with bandits.

The Kid went in boldly enough, but his

carbine was across his lap and cocked just the same. The Mexican, an enormously ugly man with his one black eye bright with unasked questions and unblinking fidelity to detail, smiled very slowly, saying nothing, waiting for the Kid to speak first.

"I am hungry."

"I am not surprised," the Mexican answered sharply, his smile broadening. "Most of us are, sooner or later. You ride a good horse, Senor."

The Kid ignored the compliment. "You have food?"

"Of course; I'll get you some."

The Mexican was turning away when the Kid stopped him. "Wait; we'll go into the house together." He swung down with the wry sound of the Mexican's laughter in his ears.

"You aren't trusting, Senor."

"I have no reason to be. Lead the way."

The Kid didn't make an obvious gesture with the cocked carbine but its eloquence was understood just the same. They went into the *jacal*. There was the look of a man around the place, but no woman-sign. The Mexican put out food on a rough, uneven table without speaking, then he stood back and watched the Indian. If he had an inkling who his guest was he was too wise to indicate it.

While the man had been busy with the food,

the Kid had reached inside the money belt for more coins. He held them now in his cupped left hand, studying the villainous looking Mexican, then he motioned the host around in front of him before he started to eat, laying the carbine so that the single, black eye of the weapon was directly on the Mexican's ample paunch. The food was good; he ate it all, saw the astonishment in the Mexican's eye and put his clenched fist on the far edge of the table and emptied it.

"For more food."

The Mexican stared at the money without moving. It was gold coin, not silver. American gold money, the best there was. A small fortune lay there. Obviously this *Indio* was no mean thief. No renegade Apache from over the line, or, if he was, he was the most superior Apache of all those terrible people. The black, single eye came up with great respect, replacing the tolerant smile. More food, all there was in the haphazard cupboards and shelves, came out willingly enough and loaded the little table. The Kid ate again, still saying nothing and watching his host like a hawk watches a chicken. When he was gorged he drank red wine that was tepid but tart, then he sat down on the bench for the first time and gestured for the Mexican to stand farther away.

"You are a horse thief?"

"Mother of God," the Mexican said, rolling up his one eye in startled horror, "you are very blunt, Senor. I deal in good horses."

"I see: In good American horses."

"Well — what would you? If the opportunity comes for one to make a living this close to *gringo-land,* he must needs be a fool not to apply himself, I think."

The Kid shrugged. "It's nothing to me, Senor. You can steal the gringos blind, and I'd be the last man on earth to complain or speak out against you. Horse stealing is an accomplishment more than a crime."

"You need a fresh animal?"

"No," the Kid said, "not especially, but if you have any good bred animals, brood mares that are open, I might buy some."

The Mexican motioned toward the little heap of dully shining gold coins. "For these, Senor?"

"No, that's for the food, and your silence after I ride on. I'll pay for any horses I buy."

The Mexican nodded agreeably. "My silence was purchased before you bought it, Senor. I am not given to speaking of past visits. Yours or anyone else's."

" *'Sta bueno.* Let's go look at your mares."

They went, the Mexican leading the way with a jaunty swagger that sprang directly from the sensation the Kid's gold coins lent him, from their place in his pants' pocket.

There were only five mares well bred enough to interest the Apache Kid. He bought and paid for them, lined them out ahead of his horse and let them get a short lead before he swung up, sat looking down at the one-eyed Mexican and spoke.

"Have there been any strangers in the country lately, that you know of, Senor?"

An indifferent shrug was his answer. "There are always strangers going one way or the other, this close to the border, Senor, but if you mean Rurales — no. Not for several days now." The little black eye was nearly grinning again. "There was something about a mad-dog Indian who has been killing Rurales over in Chihuahua, but I didn't hear all of it. Surely, the great Rurales have caught him by now." The sarcasm was thick enough to chew; heavy, peasant sarcasm made ten times as obvious as it had to be.

"They aren't still around, these Rurales?"

"*Quien sabe?* Who knows? I haven't seen any in days. If one wished to avoid them, it is no difficult job. One must only ride at night and keep to the ridges."

The Kid regarded the Mexican fixedly. This man knew what the Kid had discovered only at the imminent risk of his life. He would be a wily old one-eyed bandit if there ever was one, this grinning, greasy man with the field full of American horses. He nodded methodically at his late host.

"*Si.* One could avoid them easily enough — providing — one's friends along the back trail were disinclined to run to the police with news of a stranger's passing."

"*Madre de Dios, Señior Indio.* One could also get one's throat slit — or be stitched to one's bed in the night by an avenger's bullets — if one worked that way. For myself, I am a peaceable man, disinclined to look with any great favour upon *any* policeman, for reasons that, between us, need not be mentioned. If you refer to yourself as this stranger and myself as the one along the trail you have recently ridden over, don't give it another thought. My own skirts are not clean that I could, if I would, carry stories." He jammed a fleshy paw into his trouser pocket and fondled the little gold coins with probing affection.

"There is absolutely no reason for you to worry, Senor. I have your gold. If my loyalty didn't always go to those who give it to me like this, in honest dealings, then surely you must know what would happen to my neck if you were to say I had accepted this from you — providing you were an outlaw, of course."

The Kid was satisfied, although he thought

the Mexican talked too much. At least said more in words than he had to, to get an idea across. He, himself, didn't speak, just nodded and rode out of the yard looking ahead where the brood mares had run with their taste of freedom, then, winded, had settled down to grazing along in the general direction of the American border. He rode above them and drove them across country, westward, keeping them away from the line and toward the Sierras.

Bavispe came up over the arc of land as he went west and a little north, toward home. Here, the Apache Kid was known as a local rancher. The horses he corralled were appraised by the natives in close silence. This was homeland again. He sifted the news carefully, heard that only that very morning the surplus Rurales in the neighbourhood had returned home after an exhaustive chase of some probably mythical Indian over in Chihuahua. At any rate, whether he had been mythical or not, the flaunted Rurales hadn't caught him, and therefore those that had returned minimised the Indian's wiliness to the huge — silent and hidden — amusement of the local people.

The Kid stayed in Bavispe that night. He ate and drank, ate and drank. It was the letdown that made him aware of the tremendous appetite that seemed always to nag at him. He had trouble not appearing conspicuous. The only way to do it was to eat a meal at a different place when he had the urge for more food. Finally, gorged, sated and drugged into a rich, pleasant stupor, he rented a room and went to bed.

After that his recovery was rapid enough. But he stayed in town for three days with his brood mares before he struck out for the ranch over in the Sierras. At long last the Apache Kid was returned to the arms of his Mexican wife.

He stayed at home for the balance of the year, then, in the spring of 1895, he was back over the border again, but not as a bandit.

The trip was a leisurely one. He made a long stop at one of the old rancherias where there was a cache of Yanqui gold and plunder. He hunted and fished, staying to himself, bothering no one, enjoying the solitudes until he was ready to move, then he went down across the old familiar valleys, avoiding travelled roads and Americans, but no great effort in that direction was put forth, actually. It was simply that the Kid had learned prudence the hard way. He always learned his lessons well; profited by them. The last two lessons he bore scars to remind him of. Wallapai

Clark's marksmanship and the persistence and science of Mexico's Rurales.

He went across Arizona without a visitation en route until he came to old San Carlos, and here he spent three long days among friends. Here, too, for the last time, he talked with an old friend who had had a secret fund at his disposal to be used in apprehending the Apache Kid whom the Army didn't, it would appear, believe was dead after all, although Wallapai Clark went to his death still adamant in his personal conviction that he had killed the Kid. The old friend was Al Seiber.

The Kid waited until Seiber recognised him. He stood beside his horse like a statue, unmoving except for his eyes. Seiber looked long but showed no great surprise, only motioned toward his shade tree and sat down.

"Are you all through now, Kid?"

"Yes, I'm all through."

"That's good." Seiber seemed to be thinking of something; then he said: "That reward was withdrawn last year."

The Kid didn't answer. If he felt any embarrassment over not meeting with Seiber when Al had wanted him to, and give himself up into the old chief of scouts' custody, he made no mention of it.

"You're living in Mexico now, they tell me."

"I live there, yes, but as a citizen. A rancher, not a renegade."

"How about Kosterlitzky's Rurales? Do they know who you are?"

"*Quien sabe?* I don't know. There was a time when they almost found out, but since then I have had many Rurales stop and drink at my spring and go on. I don't think they know; if they do, they say nothing."

"A man can't be too careful — ever."

"No; I'm always careful."

"Well, Kid, I don't suppose things will ever be the same again. A man can't ever go back. All those other things are behind you. You're the only outlaw I ever knew who had sense enough to stop before it was too late. The only one."

The Kid knew that evil days were upon his old employer, but he made no mention of it. The parting was awkward because each man had a lot left unsaid within him, and wondered what, if anything, he should add to what had already been said. While each wondered, the Kid rode away. They parted forever like that. Seiber had his limp to remind him of the Apache Kid to his last day, when a boulder squashed his life out in 1907, and the Kid had memories that he carried with him across decades yet to come.

The memories may have sufficed until he

got back over to the ranch where another white man had shared a slaughtered heifer with he and Mase and some others, not too many years before.

"By Godfrey — I've heard the rumours but never believed it, Kid."

"What rumours?"

"First off that Ed Clark snaffled you; then, a few months after that ruckus died down, that you weren't dead after all. Only the Army said you were. A feller just didn't know what th' hell to believe."

The Kid laughed. "The Army's never been close enough to shoot me yet. Why would they say this man Clark — who *is* this Clark?" The dark eyes were fixed, unblinking, as steady as thick, dark mud.

"Had a friend named Diehl you are said to have killed. Will Diehl. Clark was chief of Wallapai scouts for a —"

"Where did Clark say he killed me?"

"Well — hell — a feller forgets some times. Seems to me it was down by Tombstone; don't rightly recollect. But they say this old cuss lambasted you in the head and —"

"Killed a woman."

A brief nod. "Yeah. Killed a squaw you had with you. Young girl if I remember the tale right."

The Kid's glance dropped away to the

ground, ran along to the edge of the yard where he had once talked about the Apache Kid with a red faced posseman, and lifted gently to the far horizon. "This Clark shot me in the head all right. See here? He grazed me a little and shot away that part of the ear, but he never killed me."

"Did he kill the squaw?"

"Yes. We were close enough together when he shot. I saw the bullet hit her."

"My gawd — a man's got no business killing a woman."

"He wouldn't have known it was a woman. It was dark. Besides, we were both almost flat in the grass. He wouldn't have known, I don't think. But he killed her anyway. She's dead."

There was a slight pause, then: "Well, that's one rumour a man can believe, I expect." Anxious to change the conversation, the rancher squinted in sly amusement at the Indian. "Had any beef barbecues lately? Heifer barbecues, I mean?"

The Kid's laughter was soft. "No," he said, with quick understanding. "I had to eat that one. Did you ever miss any more?"

"Not to 'Paches, far as I know. White rustlers been on the increase the last few years, but not Indians. Leastways not that I know of, and I got a fair tally, too."

"There are more rustlers up here than down in Mexico."

The white man laughed unpleasantly. "We've been a little lax in making it unhealthy for 'em hereabouts, but the boys 're getting sort of het up now. Maybe we can set up an outfit like those Rurales, and use lariat courts like they do down there." The man's eyes held to the Kid's face. "You been at San Carlos?"

"Yeah; for a few days. I got friends there. Visited for a while."

"Not on the owlhoot any more?"

"No, no more." The Kid held out a dark palm with some gold coins in it. "For that heifer."

The rancher's cheeks reddened. "I told you then —"

"I know. An Apache doesn't forget. Especially a friend. But I raise a few cattle too, now. They are the same as money. I want to pay for that one we ate. You are a good friend. I remember that."

But the rancher was adamant in his refusal to accept. There was a look of annoyance in his eyes. The Kid put the money back in his pocket and smiled, turning to his horse, gathering up the reins and toeing into the stirrup.

" 'Sta bueno, amigo; I understand. We are friends. We will always be friends."

The cowman watched him thoughtfully.

"Now what? You're going back over the line?"

"Yes. Back to the Sierra Madres. Back home. But I'll send you word so you'll know the Apache Kid is still alive and well."

And he did too, years later, when the cowman was in his yard in the early summer dusk, smoking peacefully and watching a lean, hawk-eyed man on a fine blooded horse come swinging in the lane, head turning from side to side after the fashion of all men who know no peace and carry their burden of lawlessness close to the surface, paying the price of their haunted lives by constant vigilance.

"Howdy."

The cold eyes stopped, measured the lounging cowman, appraised him quickly and unerringly, then swept out over the yard again, probing. "Evenin'. You own this place?"

"I do."

"An' — you got a friend — an Indian — you ain't seen for a long time?"

"Well, I got a lot of Indians for friends. Which one do you mean?" Now the bleak eyes stopped their roaming for a long second while the outlaw spoke a few words very distinctly and slowly, as though pulling them down out of memory with great effort. As though doing something he wasn't used to doing, saying something verbatim, just as he had been told to say it. The cowman's puzzlement vanished the first time the word "heifer" slid out. He knew who the Indian friend was now.

"Now you know who I mean, hombre?"

"Sure. You know him?"

"I reckon," the outlaw said dryly, "I been down at his place for a few weeks sort of taking a vacation. He said to come by here and deliver that message to the hombre as owned this ranch. That was all the pay he'd take for letting me cool out down there."

"Cheap enough," the cowman said.

But the outlaw's eyes showed no sardonic humour when he nodded. "Yeah. Cheap enough. Now I've paid off and I'll ride on."

"Wait a second. Hell man, it'll be nightfall in a half hour or so. Just as well light and eat and sleep a while."

"No thanks. I'll keep movin'. Got a long ride ahead of me."

The cowman shrugged. He understood. A lean lobo on the back trail. A rendezvous ahead somewhere in the shadowy forests of the highlands where others of this vulture breed would huddle and plan crimes he didn't want to know about.

The blooded horse walked fast, like any good trail horse does. The rancher watched him until the shadows lengthened, thickened and grew sombre, then he made a cigarette and smoked in the cool early evening, knowing that the Apache Kid, last of the renegade Indians to fight their losing battle with progress, was still safe and comfortable somewhere below the border in Mexico. It was a good thing to know because the men who lived in isolated places hadn't always belonged to the great society of law abiding folks, and it was hard to shake off the sympathy one felt for some outlaws. Not the kind that brought the message. Those that robbed and killed with icy eyes and no thought of why they did illegal things. But for those that had come to kill, be hunted, hounded and hated, persecuted and gunned for without a pause; those that came to their deadly estate through the circumstances that originally drove the Apache Kid to take up the hate trail. The highroad of vengeance. The hatchet of retribution. Of the Kid's kind there were many men in Arizona — all over the West, not just the Southwest — who knew and understood. The cowman was one.

After the Kid sent that message, he became a legend that the Army had said was killed by Wallapai Clark. For once though, it wasn't the everlasting same old story of Robin Hoods never dying; living on into history forever until they were reluctantly lowered into imaginative graves by even the most hard-headed of believers, when they passed the century mark. Not with the Apache Kid, who had aroused a nation while he held to his lone trail of war, for Emilio Kosterlitzky himself said later that the Apache Kid was a resident of Mexico. A law abiding rancher who paid his bills like less spectacular men, and had a family. He said he knew who the Kid was and watched him constantly, but that he would not move against him so long as the Indian obeyed the law and stayed to the narrow trail of conformance. He also said that, as long as the Apache Kid was declared "officially dead" by the United States Army, then why resurrect the past and stir up more trouble by arresting and prosecuting him?

Aside from the trouble that certainly would ensue, should the Apache Kid be persecuted for past crimes — most of which had been committed over the line anyway — and risk another uprising among all Apaches, and certainly stir up the old, dormant fires of animosity among segments of the Apache fighting men again, especially the younger, restless ones, it would be better to leave the Kid alone.

The Kid knew none of this, or if he did, it is possible that he only smiled thinly and ignored it, for Kosterlitzky's Rurales had also paid a high price for their last brush with the renegade, and evidently never knew whom they were chasing. It is inconceivable that the Russian naval deserter wouldn't have carried his extermination policy to the Kid's threshold had he known who that mysterious Indian was who out-fought and out-manoeuvred his select manhunters, leaving the Spanish-Mexican dead under a pitiless sun, along with others of the brigand crew who wore his mantle of constabulary respectability.

The Apache Kid visited friends up in Arizona again, in 1940. He was a withered little shadow of a man. Lean and mummified, as active as most old Apaches, dehydrated, devoid of surplus fat, not terribly old, as Indians go (Nana, another famous Apache warrior, was raising hell and propping it up with his band of raiders at over eighty years of age) and there was no mistaking that quick smile. The grin that had been snuffed out for almost a decade by a life of danger, and that had grown back slowly over the years, nourished by the quick, spontaneous laughter of sons that grew strong and learned the old tricks from their father.

The Apache Kid was only a story to many of the old San Carlos Indians who heard his name whispered among their parents now. An Apache legend of the lone warrior who carried on after Geronimo had been forced to quit. Who rode circles around the white men, made fools of them time and time again. A shred of the yesterdays when the old racial pride was still strong. A legend every one of the vanquished old-timers nursed close to his breast and chuckled over, knowing that, in the very last of the bitter contests, the Apache nation had finally emerged triumphant over their endless hordes of conquerors. The Apache Kid had never been captured, never been run down or beaten, never been shot down or hung high by the new owners of the old land.

When the Kid visited old friends in 1940 it was for the last time. He knew it and they knew it. There was one pursuit he couldn't out-distance; the years. So he spent twelve long days going among the old ones, finding a few, a pitifully few, who still knew him. Among the whites there were none left who could look into the rheumy old eyes and recognise anything that had struck terror into the hearts of their folks decades before. Just another old pepper-belly In'yun; you could always tell 'em, they wore Messican slippers, or something. Greaser dress, a lot of silver — there was a difference from the American Apaches all right. Just some old grandfather come over the line to renew acquaintances. An ugly old withered carcass.

The Kid rode back over the scored desert

where serpentine lines of macadam and concrete spanned the ancient bosom of his birthland, using old trails dimly recalled. He stopped once to listen to an old Apache faggot carrier tell about a monument to Al Seiber, dead now almost thirty-five years, that it was rumoured someone was going to erect. They laughed together over that. After the Army fired Seiber for his complaints against the way the Indians were treated. They smiled and wagged their heads. The people were different now too, like the desert was, and the waterholes, and even the stunted, culled-out game that was left for the hunters. A stone for Al Seiber now that he was dead. Nothing in the way of decent treatment to soften his last days, while he was alive. People changed too, evidently.

The Kid kept to his trails and came at long last to a prosperous ranch where underground water had come swelling out of the womb of the desert and been bent to man's will. It made the hot days smell much cooler too, all that harnessed water. But the steel fence around another grave was rusting, although there were no weeds inside, around the old-fashioned mound of heavy cement white men used to put over their departed fathers. The heavy thing that must make the man beneath it groan in agony, when he tried to breathe or move.

He wondered if that sleeping cowman under his impressive roll of cement ever got his message. Instinctively he knew that he had. Even outlaws, years back, kept their words. People had changed a lot now.

He looked down at the lonely little grave and memory came back of a fearless young rancher riding down to eat one of his own beeves with a wild-eyed brood of deadly renegade Apaches. It wasn't so long ago to the Kid; it was a vague sort of yesterday, true, but he could see that wry look when the cowboy said he'd eat on his horse. He recalled their conversation in '95, too. He was still standing there when a thick-set white man, young but squint-eyed and open-faced looking, came up, staring at the old Indian, towering over him, hiding the condescension very well.

"Howdy. You one of those Indians my grandfather used to tell us about? One of those old-timers he used to know?"

"Yes. I knew the man who sleeps under that pile of stone."

"Never knew him, myself, but my dad's told us a lot of the yarns the old gent used to spin. Must've been quite a lad in his day."

The Kid turned and studied the sleek, firm flesh with its well fed solidness. Its patent tolerance that was more like patronage. He said nothing, just turned and swung back into the saddle, cast another long look at the grave and rode away. Sometimes a man just lives too damned long. Sometimes he sees things that he shouldn't be allowed to see. All these nice round people with their imprecations against the desert heat, their quick talk, without thinking beforehand. People change. It was like looking into the privacy of someone else's house and seeing them naked, this living too long. Seeing things no man from the old days should be allowed to see. The Kid went back to Mexico, avoiding the travelled routes, finding no thrill in avoiding the planes overhead and the radio equipped jeeps and closely confined horse patrols that were a match for the changed people of both races who didn't know how to get across the line any more, unless they could do it with cars or airplanes. People change — and sometimes men just live too long.

The Kid died sometime during the Second World War. There is conflict about the date. But he is dead now, and only three old Apaches still live who were children when he was at his zenith, but they remember how a stranger, a Mexican Apache, came and visited their grandparents before the oldsters passed away. They were told who he was, but now he is dead, the last of the acknowledged, full fledged fighting bucks — the old bronko Apaches — and the only one who ever went out on the war trail and fought until he quit, without ever being captured or run to earth by all the forces of two great nations. The United States and Mexico. And yet he isn't hardly known of outside the hearts of his people, where he still lives as something they can point to with pride. The unconquerable Apache.

Lauran Paine who, under his own name and various pseudonyms has written over 900 books, was born in Duluth, Minnesota, a descendant of the Revolutionary War patriot and author, Thomas Paine. His family moved to California when he was at an early age and his apprenticeship as a Western writer came about through the years he spent in the livestock trade, rodeos, and even motion pictures where he served as an extra because of his expert horsemanship in several films starring movie cowboy Johnny Mack Brown. In the late 1930s, Paine trapped wild horses in northern Arizona and even, for a time, worked as a professional farrier. Paine came to know the Old West through the eyes of many who had been born in the previous century and he learned that Western life had been very different from the way it was portrayed on the screen. "I knew men who had killed other men," he later recalled. "But they were the exceptions. Prior to and during the Depression, people were just too busy eking out an existence to indulge in Saturday-night brawls." He served in the U.S. Navy in the Second World War and began writing for Western pulp magazines following his discharge. It is interesting to note that all of his earliest novels (written under his own name and the pseudonym Mark Carrel) were published in the British market and he soon had as strong a following in that country as in the United States. Paine's Western fiction is characterized by strong plots, authenticity, an apparently effortless ability to construct situation and character, and a preference for building his stories upon a solid foundation of historical fact. ADOBE EMPIRE (1956), one of his best novels, is a fictionalized account of the last twenty years in the life of trader William Bent and, in an off-trail way, has a melancholy, bittersweet texture that is not easily forgotten. MOON PRAIRIE (1950), first published in the United States in 1994, is a memorable story set during the mountain man period of the frontier. In later novels such as THE HOMESTEADERS (1986) or THE OPEN RANGE MEN (1990), he showed that the special magic and power of his stories and characters had only matured along with his basic themes of changing times, changing attitudes, learning from experience, respecting nature, and the yearning for a simpler, more moderate way of life.

We hope you have enjoyed this Large Print book. Other Thorndike Press or Chivers Press Large Print books are available at your library or directly from the publishers. For more information about current and upcoming titles, please call or write, without obligation, to:

Thorndike Press
P.O. Box 159
Thorndike, Maine 04986
USA
Tel. (800) 223-6121 (U.S. & Canada)
In Maine call collect: (207) 948-2962

OR

Chivers Press Limited
Windsor Bridge Road
Bath BA2 3AX
England
Tel. (0225) 335336

All our Large Print titles are designed for easy reading, and all our books are made to last.